"You're too good to be true. It must be an act."

"Awww, Nina." His hand slid up to cup her face. "People can be genuine."

She couldn't help but be enticed by the promise in Alex's eyes. Yet pain from past betrayals welled up, how her husband and her in-laws had so deeply let her down, worse yet how they let down precious Cody. "They can. But they usually aren't."

He stroked back her hair, tucking it behind her ear. "Then why are you even considering having dinner with me?"

"I honestly don't know." Her scalp tingled from the light brush of his fingers, his nearness overriding boundaries she thought were firmly in place.

Their gazes met, eyes held. She breathed him in, remembering the feel of his lips on hers.

Would he kiss her again? Because if he did, she wasn't sure she could say no to anything.

* * *

Pursued by the Rich Rancher is part of the Diamonds in the Rough trilogy: The McNair cousins must pass their grandmother's tests to inherit their fortune—and find true love!

Dear Reader,

I'm an author who plots stories and series way in advance of writing, but Alex McNair threw me a curveball. I knew he would fall for a single mom. However I didn't realize until the story came from my fingers that the child would have autism. That plot element came to me through an experience pairing a young boy with autism with a service dog in training—a dog I fostered through the shelter where I volunteer. Watching their special bond grow touched my heart beyond measure. After researching more on equine therapy, I knew I'd found the fit for this cowboy story.

If you missed the first Diamonds in the Rough book, *One Good Cowboy*, it's still available. The trilogy completes next month with *Pregnant by the Cowboy CEO*.

Thank you so much to all my readers for your continued support and notes. I love hearing from you online. I truly believe I am one of the luckiest authors on the planet to have such a supportive and fun group of fans!

Cheers,

Cathy

Catherine Mann

CatherineMann.com

Facebook.com/CatherineMannAuthor

Twitter.com/CatherineMann1

PURSUED BY THE RICH RANCHER

CATHERINE MANN

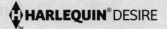

Recycling programs
for this product may
not exist in your area.

ISBN-13: 978-0-373-73392-7

Pursued by the Rich Rancher

Copyright © 2015 by Catherine Mann

Printed in U.S.A.

www.Harlequin.com

USA TODAY bestselling author **Catherine Mann** lives on a sunny Florida beach with her flyboy husband and their four children. With more than forty books in print in over twenty countries, she has also celebrated wins for both a RITA® Award and a Booksellers' Best Award. Catherine enjoys chatting with readers online—thanks to the wonders of the internet, which allows her to network with her laptop by the water! Contact Catherine through her website, catherinemann.com, find her on Facebook and Twitter (@CatherineMann1), or reach her by snail mail at PO Box 6065, Navarre, FL 32566.

Books by Catherine Mann

HARLEQUIN DESIRE

Acquired: The CEO's Small-Town Bride
Billionaire's Jet Set Babies
Honorable Intentions

The Alpha Brotherhood

An Inconvenient Affair
All or Nothing
Playing for Keeps
Yuletide Baby Surprise
For the Sake of Their Son

Texas Cattleman's Club: After the Storm

Sheltered by the Millionaire

Diamonds in the Rough

One Good Cowboy
Pursued by the Rich Rancher

Visit the Author Profile page at Harlequin.com, or catherinemann.com, for more titles.

To Mustang and his special boy. Thank you for changing my life and touching my heart.

One

Nina Lowery just didn't get the cowboy craze.

Good thing she lived in Texas. All the cowboys made it easy to resist falling for any man after her marriage combusted. And never had she been more neck deep in cowboys than today as she accompanied her son to the week-long HorsePower Cowkid Camp.

Nina peeled the back off the name tag and stuck it to her yellow plaid shirt that was every bit as new as her boots. She knelt in front of her four-year-old son and held out the tiny vest with his name stitched on it.

"Cody, you need to wear this so everybody knows which group you're with. We don't want you to get lost. Okay?"

Silently staring, Cody kept his eyes on the ground, so she had a perfect view of the top of his blond buzz cut. He lifted his hands just a hint, which she took as the okay to slide his spindly arms through the vest, leather fringe fanning in the wind. The summer smell of freshly mown hay mixed with the sticky little boy sweetness of perspiration and maple syrup from his breakfast pancakes. Cody had them every morning. Without fail.

They'd been running late today, so he'd eaten his breakfast in the car, dipping his pancake in a cup of syrup. Most of which drizzled all over his car seat. But after waking up at 4:00 a.m. to get ready, then driving from San Antonio to Fort Worth, she was too frazzled to deal with the fallout of disrupting any more of his daily routine. Syrup could be cleaned later.

There were far tougher issues to tackle in bringing up Cody than combating a trail of ants.

She would do anything for her little boy. Anything. Including immersing herself in the world of boots and spurs for seven days. *Yeehaw.*

About a month ago, when her four-year-old's eyes had lit up during a field trip to a farm, she'd been taken aback. He'd been mesmerized by the horses. So Nina had devoted herself to becoming an expert on all things equine related, desperate for a means to break through the walls surrounding her autistic son.

Finding a pathway of communication was rare and cherished when parenting a child with autism.

Never in a million years would she have guessed this particular world would pique Cody's interest. Usually boisterous encounters spun him up, leaving him disoriented and agitated. Sometimes even screaming. Rocking. His little body working overtime to block the excess stimuli.

But he liked it here. She could tell from his focus and the lack of tension in his body. She'd only seen him this way while drawing. He was a little savant with crayons and paint, finding creative canvases from rocks to boxes and, yes, walls. She even had a Monet-esque flower mural down her hall.

Apparently he was a horse savant, as well.

She held out the pint-size straw hat and let him decide whether or not he wanted to take it from her to wear. Textures were an iffy proposition for him. The brush of a rough fabric could send him into sensory overload, especially on a day when there were already so many new sights and sounds, horses and humans everywhere. She sidestepped to make way for a father pushing his daughter in a wheelchair, the tyke's arms in the air as she squealed, "Giddyap, Daddy!"

Cody clutched his tiny Stetson in his hands until a long-legged ranch hand strutted past. Standing straight, his eyes tracking the man walking away, her son slid his hat in place and tilted it to the side just like the stable hand he watched. Nina breathed a sigh of relief. She'd made the right decision to come here.

The cowboy camp for special-needs kids was a clear fit for her son. The program had only started this summer, but was already receiving high acclaim. The wealthy McNair family had put their power, influence and money behind launching HorsePower Cowkid Camp on their hobby ranch—Hidden Gem. The bulk of their fortune, though, had been made in their jewelry design house that created rustic Western styles.

Cody toyed with the fringe on his vest, tracing the stamped jewel patterns imprinted in the leather. She reminded herself to stay cautiously optimistic. They'd only just arrived.

She'd learned long ago not to set unrealistic expectations. Life worked better when she celebrated individual moments of success, such as how Cody took steps toward that cowboy. A horse whinnied and her son smiled. That meant more than the hundreds of hugs she would never get.

"Cody, let's walk around and explore. We have a couple of hours to settle in before the first activity." She was used to rambling on to fill the silences. Her son did speak. Just not often. Rather than expecting Cody to answer, she was advised by the speech therapist to accept it as a pleasant surprise when he did and take heart in his advanced vocabulary choices.

Cody held up his hand for her to take and she linked her fingers around his. A rare reach-out. Her heart filled at the chance to touch her child. If Cody wanted the ranch experience, she would follow that broad-shouldered cowboy to the ends of the earth.

Weaving around the other families, she tried not to notice how many of the children were accompanied by two parents. She savored the feel of her son's hand in hers and charged ahead to a corral about ten yards away, on the periphery of the camper chaos.

Multiple barns, cabins and corrals were walking distance from the lodge. Some would call the lodge a mansion—a rustic log ranch mansion with two wings. One wing for vacationers, the other wing for the McNairs' personal living quarters. The place had expanded from a B & B to a true hobby ranch, with everything from horseback riding to a spa, fishing and trail adventures... even saloon-style poker games. They catered to a variety of people's needs, from tourists to weddings.

And now this special needs kids' camp, as well.

She refused to be wowed by the family's power.

She'd walked that path, been too easily blinded by her ex's charm. The thought of a wealthy life of ease with a handsome guy had seemed like a fairy tale and so she'd seen what she wanted to see. But her would-be prince had definitely turned into a toad, taking that fairy-tale ending with him.

Nina skirted past a half dozen children surrounding a rodeo clown passing out toy horses. Childish squeals filled the air.

"I wanna spotted pony."

"Please, please the brown one with a girl rider."

"I wike the one wiff sparkles on the saddle!"

Cody, however, kept his eyes on the cowboy. For the most part, she'd only seen chaps on men in after-shave commercials. Even in Texas they weren't common. This guy's leathers were dusty and worn, the type a man wore to work. A real man. Not an overindulged toad prince like her ex.

So okay, maybe there was something to be said for the cowboy appeal after all.

Cody's cowboy leaped over the split-rail fence in a smooth blend of instinct and strength, his tan Stetson staying firmly in place. He walked with loose-hipped confidence toward a wild horse pawing the ground, nostrils flaring. The animal clearly didn't like the saddle on his back and eyed the approaching man with wariness. The horse danced nervously, shifting uneasy weight from hindquarter to hindquarter, powerful muscles flexing. She felt her son's pulse kick in excitement. So in spite of the tremor of fear in her heart, she stepped closer to the corral.

She'd been thrown once as a child and hadn't been

a fan of horses since then. She liked to think she was a person who learned her lesson. Once burned. Twice shy.

Yet the man in front of her showed no fear as he spoke softly to the stressed beast, lulling with his hypnotic voice and gentle strokes. Her stomach gripped just as he slid onto the horse's back.

Pinning his ears back, the horse yanked hard on the reins. Now the animal was well and truly pissed.

Cody tugged his hand free. "Let go."

And she only then realized she'd been squeezing too hard. "Sorry, sweetie."

"Uh-huh." Her son walked closer to the fence, and a different fear took over. Her child had very little sense of danger.

She stifled her own anxiety and stepped closer. "Cody, we have to stay outside the fence to watch. We can't go inside and disturb the man's work."

"Kay…" Her son nodded, enraptured.

The cowboy urged the horse gently forward. The horse bucked hard but had no luck at unseating the skilled rider. His cowboy hat, however, went flying. The midmorning sun glinted off his head of thick black hair.

The kind of hair a woman could run her fingers through.

The wayward thought hit her as hard and fast as those hooves pounding the ground. She'd never bought into cowboy lore, especially after being tossed on her butt by that supposedly docile pony. Until now. At this moment, she couldn't take her eyes off the smooth flow of the ranch hand's body as he became one with the horse. He rode the frenzy without letting it take control of him, rolling naturally with the unpredictable movements. She understood the restraint and self-control it took to tap in to that Zen state in the face of such outright terror.

She carried fears of her own. Of not being able to care for her son as a single parent. Of trusting a man again after the hell and betrayal her ex-husband had put her through before their breakup and then his death in a motorcycle accident.

Those fears were nothing compared to the terrors her son faced. And the roadblocks.

Somehow she could tell this cowboy understood that fear. Knew how to ride through the moment until peace returned. He had the well-being of the horse in his care in mind at all times. And Cody was mesmerized.

So was she.

Finally—she had no idea how long they stood watching—the horse settled into a restless trot, circling the fenced area, snorting. Nina exhaled in a rush, only just now realizing she'd been holding her breath and secretly rooting for him.

Cody knelt down and picked up the man's hat, shook off the dust and held it out. "Mister. Your Stetson."

Her son's voice came out a little raspy from being used so infrequently. The cowboy tipped his face toward them, the sunshine streaming over…

Oh my.

He'd stepped right off some Wild West movie poster and into her reality. High, strong cheekbones and a square jaw, damn good-looking *power.* She blinked fast against the sting of dust in the air.

He guided the horse to their side of the fence, and her stomach flipped. Because of close proximity to the horse, right?

Ha.

She'd quit lying to herself a long time ago.

The cowboy dipped closer, extending an arm toward Cody. "Thank you, little man." His voice was like Southern Comfort on the rocks, smooth with a nip. "I'm guessing by that vest you're here for camp. Are you having fun?"

"Uh-huh." Cody nodded without making eye contact. "Spectac-u-lar."

Would the man understand? This was a special needs camp, after all.

The cowboy stroked a hand along the horse's neck. "I see you like Diamond Gem. He's a good horse, but too large for you. The camp counselors will start you out with pony rides and before you know it you'll be ready for the big leagues."

Cody shuffled his feet and tugged at the fringe on his vest.

"Thank you," Nina said. "Cody's not very talkative, but he understands all we're saying."

He looked at her, his eyes laser blue. A shiver of awareness tingled through her. Did all of him have to be so damn charismatic?

A dimple tucked into one of his cheeks. "I'm usually not much of a chatty guy myself, actually."

He'd done better with Cody today than her ex-husband ever had. Warren had been a charmer, sweeping her off her feet with extravagant gestures, making her believe in the fairy-tale ending right up until...*ribbit*. Warren was a shallow, spoiled mama's boy with too much money and too little ambition other than the next thrill. When life got real, when the day-to-day specifics of dealing with their son's autism added up, he'd checked out on the marriage. Then he'd checked out on life altogether in his reckless motorcycle accident.

Cody scuffed his little boots in the dirt, his mouth moving, repeating, "Rodeo man, rodeo man."

The cowboy dipped his head, then nodded. "Back in the day, I was. Not any longer."

Cody went silent, and Nina scrambled for something to say. For her son's sake, of course, not because she wanted another taste of that Southern Comfort drawl saturating her senses. "Then what was that show all about?"

"Just doing my job, ma'am. This was actually a low-key session," he said, his voice washing over her as he sat astride the horse, his muscular thighs at eye level... and his hips. Diamond Gem shook his head up and down, shaking the reins, a reminder that the horse, although calm now, was still unsettled. "Diamond Gem and I have been working together for a couple of weeks."

That was an *easy* session?

"Do you miss the rodeo days?" she found herself asking, unable to stop herself from thinking of all the regrets Warren had lamented over after settling down.

The dusty cowboy scratched under his hat, then settled it back in place. "Let's just say these days I prefer to spend my time communing with the animals rather than performing for people."

"And this horse? You were communing?"

"This fella was confiscated by local animal control for neglect and..." He glanced at her son. "And for other reasons. Releasing him into the wild where he would be unable to fend for himself wasn't an option. So he came here to us where we can socialize him. He's a little green and gun-shy, but we've made progress."

So he'd used the old skills to help this horse. Was he playing on her heartstrings as a part of some camp gimmick or was he as genuine as those blue eyes? She settled on saying, "That's admirable of you to risk breaking a rib—or worse—to help the horse."

The dimple twitched at his cheek again. "I may have enjoyed myself a little bit…" His eyes dipped down to the name tag stuck to her shirt. "Nina."

Her skin prickled and heat flushed through her at the sound of her name coated in those whiskey tones. What harm was there in indulging in a light flirtation with a regular guy? No risk. She was only here for a week. Although she could be imagining his interest.

It was probably just his job as an employee to be polite to the customers.

"Well, my son certainly enjoyed it, as well. Thank you." She backed up a step. "We should start unpacking or we'll miss the lunch kickoff."

"Wouldn't want that to happen." He touched the brim of his hat. "Y'all have a nice time at the HorsePower Cowkid Camp."

Her skin flushed, heating at the sound of his low and rumbly voice soothing ragged nerves. How strange to be lulled and turned on all at once. But God, how she craved peace in her life. She treasured it in a way she never would have guessed a decade ago.

And watching the lumbering cowboy ride away, she had a very real sense of how smooth and sexy could coexist very, very well in one hot package.

For the first time in months, Alex McNair was stoked about the possibility of asking out a woman. He'd been telling himself for months he needed to move on after his cousin got engaged to the only woman Alex had ever wanted to marry. But the one-night stands he'd been having lately didn't count as moving forward with his life.

He slung the saddle off Diamond Gem's back and passed it over to a stable hand. Diamond Gem looked sideways at Alex from the cross ties and let out a long nicker. He preferred to brush and settle his own horses, but his responsibilities overseeing the Hidden Gem Ranch interfered more often than not with that simple work these days. He missed free time in the saddle, but his MBA was needed here more than his equestrian skills.

And the number-one priority today? He was due to meet his grandmother for an early lunch. That took precedence over anything else. He didn't know how many more meals they would share, since she had terminal brain cancer.

With his grandmother's illness, he had to step up to fill the huge void left by their McNair matriarch. Which probably made this a bad time to think about starting a relationship, even a short-term one, but the woman—Nina—intrigued him. Her curly red hair and soft curves snagged his attention, and the memory of her berry scent lingered in his senses.

And the protective way she watched over her son drew him in at a time when his emotions were damn raw. He didn't want to overanalyze why she pulled at him. He was just glad as hell for the feeling.

It had taken him a long while to get over the fact that his cousin would be marrying Johanna. But he'd gotten past that. He had to. She would be in the family forever now. Family was too important for any kind of awkwardness to linger.

The family needed to stick together, especially with their grandmother's cancer. They needed to support her, and had to make sure the McNair empire ran smoothly through this time of transition. Giving their grandmother peace during her final days was their most important task.

Still, he couldn't stop thinking about the woman— Nina. He didn't even know her last name, for God's sake, but he sure intended to find out. He could see asking her to accompany him to his cousin's wedding. How far did she live from here? People came from all over for the camp, but the bulk were local.

Regardless, distance didn't really matter. Not to a McNair. He had the family plane at his disposal. And yet all that money couldn't give them the one thing each of them really wanted.

Their grandmother's health.

He strode toward the main house, veering off to the family's wing where he was to meet his grandmother on the porch. His boots crunched along pine straw, children's chatter and a banjo playing echoed in the distance. Branches rustled overhead. Some of those oak trees were older than him and he'd climbed those thick branches as a kid.

He neared the family porch where his grandmother— Mariah McNair—already sat in a rocking chair. A tray of sandwiches and a pitcher of tea waited on the table between the two rockers.

His gut knotted with dread over the day that rocker would be empty.

Her favored jean jumper and boots fit her more

loosely these days. And her hair was shorter now. For as long as he could remember, she'd worn it long, either in a braid down her back or wrapped in a bun on her head. But she'd undergone a procedure to drain blood buildup in her head a few months ago. Her hair had been cut short and shaved away at the surgery site.

That made it real for him. She was going to die sooner rather than later, and not of old age. That damn tumor was going to steal her from them.

"You made it," she said, clapping her hands. "Come sit beside me, load up a plate and let's talk."

"I'll clean up and be right back down." He worried about her getting sick on top of everything else.

"Now is better. A little dust and dirt isn't going to make me keel over. Besides, I've seen you messier."

"That you have." He swept off his hat and hunkered down into the rocker beside her, resting his hat on his knee, thinking of how cute that kid Cody had looked passing it back to him. "How are you feeling, Gran? Do you want more tea?"

He reached for the pitcher, noticing she'd only nibbled at the corner of a sandwich.

"I'm fine, Alex, thank you. I have the sunshine, a glass of sweet tea and one of my grandchildren here. All is right in my world."

But he knew that wasn't really true. She didn't have long to live. Months. Maybe only weeks. She'd been getting her affairs in order, deciding who would inherit what. Not that he cared a damn thing about the McNair wealth and holdings. He just wanted his grandmother.

He reached for a plate and piled on sandwiches, more to make her happy. His stomach felt as if it had rocks in it right now. "Thanks for lunch. It's a chaotic day with all the campers coming in."

"Stone surprised us all by starting that camp instead of taking over the jewelry enterprises, but in a good way."

Alex touched his hat on his knee. "That he did."

"His new life fits him. Johanna helped him see that path while she helped him with his inheritance test." Mariah set her plate of uneaten sandwiches aside. "Alex, I want to talk to you about *your* test."

"*My* test?" The rocks in his stomach turned icy. "I thought that was just a game to get Stone and Johanna back together."

At least he'd hoped so as time passed and his grandmother didn't bring up the subject of putting her three grandchildren through an arbitrary test to win their portion of the estate.

It wasn't about the money. It was about the land. A mega-resort developer simply could not get a hold of Alex's portion of the land. That, he definitely cared about.

"Well, Alex, you thought wrong. I need to feel secure about the future of what we've built. All three of you children have a stubborn streak."

"One we inherited from you."

"True enough." She laughed softly before her blue eyes turned sad. "Much more so than my two children."

Her daughter had been a junkie who dropped her child—Stone—off onto Mariah's doorstep. Alex and his twin Amie's father had been unmotivated to do more than spend his inheritance and avoid his wife.

Mariah had been more of a parent to Alex than his own.

He, Amie and Stone were like siblings, having grown

up here at Hidden Gem together. Once they'd finished college, they all turned their attention to home, working to keep the McNair holdings profitable even after their grandfather died. Each one of them had a role to play. Alex managed the family lands—Hidden Gem Ranch, which operated as a bed-and-breakfast hobby ranch for the rich and famous. Until recently, Stone had managed the family jewelry design house and store. Diamonds in the Rough featured high-end rustic designs, from rodeo belt buckles and stylized bolos to Aztec jewelry, all highly sought after around the country. And Amie—a gemologist—created most of their renowned designs, even though the McNair jewelry company was now under new management, an outsider his grandmother had hired.

Gran rocked slowly, sipping her iced tea, her hand thin and pale with spidery veins as she set the glass back on the table between them. "Now back to what I've planned for your test."

That damn test again. Stone had already passed his test to retain control of the jewelry business. Gran had made Stone work with Johanna to find loving homes for his grandmother's dogs. Yet once Stone had finished, he surprised them all by proposing to Johanna and announcing he didn't want to run Diamonds in the Rough after all. He didn't want the all-consuming ambition. The camp had been Stone's brainchild, shifting his focus to the family's charity foundation, investing his portion of the estate into a self-generating fund to run the HorsePower program while a new CEO assumed command as head of Diamonds in the Rough.

"Seriously, Gran? You're still insisting on the test? I assumed since Stone backed out and opted to live on his own portfolio you would pass the company along to Amie."

"And leave the running of the ranch to you?"

He stayed silent. The land. This place. He'd put his heart and soul into it. But that was his grandmother's decision to make. Money wasn't a concern. He had his own. He could start fresh if need be.

Except he didn't want to. He wanted his home to stay untouched by takeover from some mega-ranch theme park.

Mariah set aside her tea. "Alex, it's a simple test really. There's a competitor—Lowery Resorts—that has been quietly buying up shares of the McNair empire through shell corporations."

Alarms went off in his head. This was the worst possible time for someone to stage a takeover. Stockholders were already on edge about his grandmother's illness, concerned about the uncertain future of the McNair holdings. "A controlling percentage?"

"Not yet. But between my illness, Stone's resignation as CEO and his replacement still gaining his footing, some investors perceive a void. If our loyalties split or if they continue consolidating, we could be at risk of having our haven turned into a sideshow resort."

How the hell had this happened? His hands gripped the arms of the chair and he resisted the urge to vent his frustration. He bit back the words he wanted to spout and simply said, "How did they manage that?"

"When word first leaked of my illness, they moved fast and took advantage of investor fears. I should have seen that coming. I trusted old friendships. I was wrong. I need to move faster now. Time's too important."

He should have seen this coming. He should have

thought beyond his part of the family holdings. "We could have Stone return as CEO until the crisis with the Lowery Resorts passes."

"No, he doesn't want it, and I need to see the company settled with our new CEO, Preston Armstrong, in control before I can rest easily. The board and I chose Preston because we believe in him, but he will need time to gain investors' trust. So in the meantime, I need your help."

"You don't need to make it a test." He patted her hand, then gripped it. "Just tell me what to do for you and I'm here for you, for the family."

Smiling, she gave his hand a squeeze back, before her eyes narrowed with the laser focus that had leveled many in the business world. "The Lowery family has a vulnerability in their portfolio."

"You want me to exploit it?" His mind churned with possibilities he wanted to discuss with Stone.

"Convince the Lowerys to sell back a sizeable portion of those shares bought by their shell companies and I'll transfer all my shares of the ranch into your hands effective immediately."

He waved aside the last part of her words. "It's not about me accumulating a larger part of the homestead. It's about our family. I will not allow our land to pass into anyone else's hands."

She nodded tightly. "There's that old competitive spirit of yours. I was wondering if you'd buried it completely under that laid-back air you carry around these days."

"Hmm." He didn't like reminders of that side of himself. He picked up his tea and drank. There was still a lot of dirt inside him to wash away from those rodeo

days. Things he'd allowed his parents to push him to
do. Things he regretted.

"You need to be aware, the Lowery family is going
to be resistant. You'll need to be careful and savvy in
gaining the trust of the one chink in their armor. I've
even given you a head start."

He paused mid-drink, then set his glass back down
carefully. "What do you mean by head start?"

Her thumbs rubbed along the arms of the wooden
rocker. "The vulnerable shares belong to the Lowery
grandson. His widowed mother is the executor, and she
needs to invest wisely for the boy's future—long-term."

A kid? A widow? A creeping sensation started up
his spine, as if he were about to get kicked by a horse or
run over by a stampede. "Gran, what have you done?"

"I investigated all the Lowerys, of course. And when
I found out the grandson adores all things cowboy, I
made sure a brochure for our camp landed in his mother's hands so we would have the chance to meet with
them—away from the grandparents' influence."

Ah, damn. It couldn't be…

"In fact, I believe you've already met her and her
son." She pointed a frail finger toward the corral, where
she would have had a clear view of his morning activities.

Crap. He could almost hear that stampede gaining
speed, ready to run him over.

"The lovely red-haired lady who watched you work
with Diamond Gem."

Two

The sun was low and warm, piercing through the barn windows as Nina sat at a long wooden table eating supper with the other parents. A country band played twangy children's songs, a group of young campers sitting clustered in front of the small stage. Cody rocked and flapped his hands in time, having already finished his macaroni and cheese. A little girl with a pink scarf over her shaved head spun in circles with a streamer. A little boy with cerebral palsy held his new friend's hand as they danced. Three children ran up to the stage clapping.

She'd spent the morning unpacking, then eating lunch and attending camp sessions with her son, followed by pony rides, arts and crafts. They'd made belts and jewelry. And not just the children, but the adults had been included, as well. She touched the bracelet full of little charms, all Wild West themed, and a gem that was also her son's birthstone.

Between the horses and the art, her son's two favorite activities, Cody had been enthralled. The tiny sticker jewels he'd glued to the belt made an intricate repeating pattern that had even surprised the instructor.

Her son was happy, but tired from a good day. The best she could remember having in a long time. And she couldn't deny that her mind wandered back to the morning and the dusty cowboy who probably hadn't given her a second thought. But she'd kept looking for him in the crowds.

And she didn't know his name.

She stabbed at her dinner salad, covered in strips of tender steak. The big grill outside had been fired up with a variety of meats, potatoes and corn for the adults. She was wondering how the fee they charged possibly covered such a high-end production. The McNair family, or some of their wealthy friends, had to be underwriting the expense. Her in-laws were always looking for tax havens. As fast as the thought hit her, she winced. She hated how cynical she'd become, but it was hard to feel sympathy for people who wanted to write a check rather than get to know their only grandchild.

Old anger and hurt simmered. She sliced through a steak strip, took a big bite and reminded herself to enjoy this great food and the break from always staying on guard as the only person to watch over Cody.

A shadow stretched across her, giving her only a second's warning to chew faster.

"Would you like some dessert?" Warm whiskey tones caressed her neck and ears.

She set her fork down carefully and swallowed the

bite before turning around. Sure enough, her dusty cowboy stood behind her, holding a plate of blueberry cobbler—except he wasn't dusty any longer.

His chaps and vest were gone. Just fresh jeans and a plaid shirt with the sleeves rolled up. Her eyes were drawn to the sprinkling of dark hair along his tanned forearms. Masculine arms. Funny how she'd forgotten how enticing such details could be.

"Oh, hello, again." Why had she thought she wasn't attracted to cowboys?

"Dessert?"

She shook herself out of the fog before she embarrassed herself. "Not just yet, thank you. I'm stuffed from supper. I didn't expect the meal to be this good, so I snacked earlier."

He straddled the bench, sitting beside her. "What did you expect? Rubber chicken?"

The hint of man musk and aftershave reminded her of how long it had been since she'd had a man in her life. In her bed.

Shrugging, she twirled her fork in the sparse remains of her salad. "I thought since this is a kiddie camp, the cuisine would be all about catering to their finicky palates. And there certainly was plenty for my son to pick from. I just didn't think there would be such a lavish adult course, as well."

"Gotta keep the parents happy too if we want repeat customers." He cut the spoon through the cobbler and scooped a bite, his electric blue eyes on her the whole time.

She shivered with awareness. And she wasn't the only woman noticing. More than one mom cast an envious look her way.

"True enough. Well, um, thank you for checking on us…" Was this standard for all the customers? Something in his eyes told her otherwise. "I still don't know your name."

"Sorry about that. How rude of me." He held out his hand. "My name's Alex."

He said it with an intensity that made her wonder if she was missing something.

Shaking off the sensation, she folded his hand in hers and held back the urge to shiver at the feel of masculine skin, delicious. "Hello, Alex, I'm not sure if you remember but I'm Nina and my son is Cody."

"I remember," he said simply. "But it's still nice to meet you both. Officially."

She eased her hand from his before she made a fool of herself. "You must be tired after a full day of work."

"Truth be told, I'd have rather had more time outdoors rather than spend the afternoon at a desk."

A desk? She'd assumed…well, there were lots of jobs on a ranch. She should know better than to judge by appearances. It was better to get to the heart, the truth, straightaway. She glanced at Cody. "My son has autism, if you didn't already guess."

This was usually the point where people said something about being sorry and how they knew a friend who had a friend who had a kid with autism, and then they left. And that was the reason she made a point to blurt it out early on, to weed out the wheat from the chaff. Life was mostly full of chaff.

He mixed some blueberries with the vanilla ice cream and brought the spoon to his mouth. "You don't have to explain to me."

"Most people are curious and I can't help feeling the

need to tell you before Cody has one of his meltdowns." She wet her mouth with a quick sip of tea. "It's easier when people understand why."

"This camp is here to do what's easier for him, not easier for us."

His words surprised her, warmed her. "Thank you. That approach is rarer than you would think."

"Since Stone put this camp together, we've all become more enlightened." He dug into the crust covered in blueberries.

"This place is amazing, and it's only day one. I can't believe how much fun I had and how much I'm already looking forward to tomorrow."

He eyed her over his raised spoon. "You sound surprised."

"I hope you won't take this the wrong way." She picked at the knee of her jeans. "But I'm not much of a cowgirl."

"Really? I never would have guessed," he said dryly.

"What gave me away?"

"What didn't?" He pointed to her feet. "New boots."

"New shirt too." She toyed with the collar. "I'm trying to fit in for Cody's sake, but apparently I'm not pulling it off as well as I thought."

"You're here for your kid, helping him pursue his own interests. That's nice, no matter what you're wearing." His eyes held hers, launching a fresh shower of sparks shimmering through her.

Then he blinked and stood. Regret stung over his leaving, which was silly because she was only here for a week. It wasn't as if they were going to have any kind of relationship. Her focus should be her son. Just because this cowboy seemed down-to-earth and uncomplicated didn't mean a thing. Not in the long run.

He glanced back over his shoulder at her, and her thoughts scattered.

"Nina, it would be a real shame for you to miss out on the Hidden Gem's blueberry cobbler. How about I bring some by this evening?" He held up a hand. "And before you accuse me of being some cowboy Casanova with ulterior motives, we'll stay out on the porch where you can hear your son if he wakes up. And the porch will be very public, so there's no cause to worry about me making a move."

"Does this kind of service always come with the camp registration?"

"No, ma'am. This is just for you." He tipped his hat. "I'll see you at nine tonight."

He didn't have a plan yet on how to persuade Nina Lowery to sell her stocks to him. He was going on instinct with her, except right now his gut didn't want to maneuver her anywhere but to bed…or on a walk.

What the hell was his grandmother thinking bringing a woman and her special-needs son here under false pretenses? There were a dozen other ways this could have been handled, but all those honest means were no longer an option now that she was already here.

At dinner, he'd considered just coming clean with her right away. Then he'd seen her eyes light up when he'd come to sit with her. The next thing he knew, he was chatting with her, digging himself in deeper until it was going to be one heck of a tangle to get himself out. If he told her now, she would shut him down, which would be bad for his grandmother and quite frankly, bad for him. He wanted to get to know her better. Maybe if he understood her, he would know the best way to approach her.

He couldn't deny that she was skittish. That much he knew for sure, sensed it the way he sensed when a horse was about to bolt.

Damn.

She definitely wouldn't appreciate being compared to a horse, but he'd realized long ago, his instincts with animals served him well in dealing with people too. He needed to approach carefully, take his time, get a sense of her.

Learn more about her.

Then he would know how to proceed. And that didn't stop the pump of anticipation over seeing Nina. He secured the two bags in his grip—the promised dessert.

He scanned the line of cabins that held the campers. Most of the buildings were two-bedrooms. He'd searched through the paperwork to learn she was staying in number eight. Katydids buzzed a full-out Texas symphony in the quiet night, allowing only muffled sounds coming from the lodge's guest lanai. Guests had already begun to arrive for his cousin's wedding. Between them and the campers, the place would be packed by Friday.

Spare time was in short supply. Alex stood at the bottom of the three steps in front of cabin number eight, eyeing the pair of rockers on the porch, exactly the same style as the ones on his family's longer wraparound that held a half dozen rocking chairs and four porch swings.

Guilt pinched his conscience again.

His grandmother had always been a woman of honor and manners. He couldn't figure out why she'd come up with such an underhanded test for him. It just didn't make sense, and his grandmother had always been logical, methodical. Could the cancer be clouding her judgment in spite of the doctor's reassurance otherwise?

But Alex wasn't ready to lead the charge to declare her unfit. That was a step he simply couldn't take. He would ride this out, play along and hope like hell an answer came to him soon.

He stepped up the wooden stairs, his boots thudding. He rapped his knuckles on the door, not wanting to wake Nina's son. He heard her footsteps approach, pause, then walk again until there was no question that she stood just on the other side of the door. But it didn't open.

Definitely skittish.

Finally she opened the door, angling outside and making it clear he wasn't coming in. She wore the same jeans and boots from earlier but had changed into a formfitting T-shirt with "hello" in multiple languages. Her hair was free from the ponytail, flowing around her shoulders in loose red curls.

God, he could lose himself for hours running his hands through her hair, feeling it brush along his skin. "Cobbler's warm and the ice cream's still cold. Shall we sit?"

"Yes, thank you." She gestured to the rockers, studying him with a wary smile. "You didn't have to do this."

He stopped. "Do you want me to leave?"

She glanced back over her shoulder, her hair swishing, enticing. "You're already here and I wouldn't want to deny you your dessert. Have a seat." She gestured to the table between them. "I set out some iced tea."

He thought of his talk with his grandmother earlier,

the shared tea, so few moments like that left with her. "Sweet tea?"

"The kind that was waiting for me in the fridge, compliments of your staff."

"Sweet tea is Southern ambrosia." He placed the containers on the end table between the rockers.

"One of my favorite things about moving down South." She cradled the glass in her hands, those long slim fingers drawing his eyes to her.

He cleared his throat. "What brought you to Texas?"

"How do you know I'm not from another Southern state?" She set her drink aside and took the container with her dessert, spooning ice cream on top.

"I saw your application." He could confess that much at least.

Her delicate eyebrows shot up. "Is that ethical?"

"It's not illegal, and I can't deny I wanted to know more about you. I still do."

"I guess I'll forgive you. This time." She ate a bite of cobbler, a sensual *hmm* vibrating from her as she closed her eyes.

Her pleasure sent hot lava through his veins.

"For what it's worth, I didn't read much of your application." But only because he'd been interrupted. "Just enough to make sure I got the right cabin so I can learn the rest on my own, asking you, getting to know you better while you're here. Are your rooms comfortable?"

"The place is perfect. Hardly roughing it." Smiling, she dug into her dessert with gusto.

"Hidden Gem works hard to keep authenticity to the experience while providing comfort. It may be a hobby ranch, but it's not a resort." He joined her in eating even though he'd had some earlier. Sharing the food with her here in the dark night was...intimate.

"I can see the special charm of the Hidden Gem. And hear it."

"What do you mean?" He glanced at her, surprised.

"I can't believe how peaceful this place is. That's important for my son, keeping the stimuli manageable," she said matter-of-factly.

"For his autism?" he asked carefully.

"Yes, it's moderate." She nodded. "I'm sure you've noticed his verbal impairment. He's advanced academically, especially in areas of interest like art and reading. He's only four, but he can lose himself in a book. Reading soothes him, actually...I didn't mean to ramble."

"I want to know more. I apologize if I'm being too nosy."

"Not at all. I would rather people ask than harbor misconceptions, or worse yet, pass judgment without any knowledge." She sagged back in her chair, dessert container resting on her lap. "I knew something wasn't right from the start, but my ex-husband and his family insisted he was just colicky. Then his verbal skills lagged and he couldn't initiate even the most basic social interaction with other children... We had to face facts. I had get help for him even if that caused a rift with my husband."

Her maternal instincts, that mama bear ferocity, spoke to him. He admired the hell out of that, even as he realized his grandmother might well have underestimated how hard it would be to get this woman to part with those stocks unless she was 100 percent certain her son got the best end of the deal. "I'm sorry you didn't get the support you should have from Cody's father."

"Thank you." Her green eyes shadowed with pain mixed with determination. "Early intervention is so crucial. I had to be his advocate, even if the rest of the family wasn't ready to accept the truth."

He found himself asking, "And Cody's father?"

"My ex-husband sent child support payments." She set aside the foam container as if she'd lost her appetite. "But he didn't want to have anything to do with Cody."

"Sent?"

"He died in a motorcycle crash shortly after our divorce." Silence settled like a humid dark blanket of a summer night.

"I'm sorry." Such inadequate words for the mix of losses she'd suffered, not just through the death of her ex, but in how the man had let her down.

"I like to think with time he could have accepted his son and been a part of Cody's life." Her head fell back against the rocker, her red hair shifting and shimmering in the porch light. "Now we'll never have that chance."

Time, a word that was his enemy these days, with his grandmother's cancer. "Regrets are tough to live with."

And he would always regret it if he didn't help ease his grandmother's last days.

Nina shook her head quickly as if clearing her thoughts and picked up her dessert again. "Enough about me. I don't mean to sound like my life is some maudlin pity party. I have a beautiful son who I love very much. I have a great, flexible job and no financial worries. Moving on." She scooped up some berries. "Tell me about you? How did you end up working at the Hidden Gem Ranch?"

"My family has always lived here." He couldn't imagine living anywhere else, especially after spending so much of his childhood and teenage years being dragged around the country by his parents to participate in rodeos. "I guess you could say I appreciate the quiet."

"So you're a professional cowboy? Rodeos and all?"

He'd lived a whole career by eighteen thanks to his mother's obsession with trotting her kids out into competitive circles—him with rodeos and his twin sister, Amie, with pageants. "My rodeo days are long past."

"Because?"

He shrugged. "Too many broken bones."

She gasped. "How awful. Are you okay?"

"Of course. It's all in the past. Kid stuff." As a boy, he hadn't argued with his parents' insistence that he continue to compete the moment the latest cast was removed. He'd even enjoyed parts of the competition. Most of all, he'd craved his parents' attention, and that was the only reliable way to get it. But then his favorite horse had broken a leg during a competition and had to be put down. He'd lost the fire to compete that day, realizing he'd only been doing it for his parents. More than anything, he'd wanted to go home and commune with the land and his horses.

Time to change the damn subject. "What do you do in San Antonio?"

She blinked at the quick change of subject, then said, "I'm a translator. Before I married I worked in New York at the United Nations." She toyed with the Eiffel Tower charm on her simple silver necklace. "My husband worked at the stock exchange. We dated for a year, got married, moved back to his home state of Texas…" She shrugged. "Now I help translate novels for foreign editions."

Ah, the necklace and T-shirt made sense now. "What languages?"

"Spanish, French, German."

"Wow," he nodded, eyebrows lifting, "that's impressive."

She shrugged dismissively, her hand sliding back to her neck, stroking the Eiffel Tower charm. "Words are my thing just as horses and running a business are yours."

Words were her "thing," yet she had a virtually nonverbal son. "When you said you're a city girl, you weren't kidding. Do you miss the job?"

"I don't regret a thing," she said between bites of cobbler. "I'm lucky to have a job that enables me to stay home with my son. I don't have to worry about making the appointments he needs."

"What about help? Grandparents?"

"My parents help when they can, but I was a late-in-life baby for them, unplanned. They're living on a shoestring budget in a retirement community in Arizona. My ex's parents come up with different options, ranging from some cult miracle cure one week to institutionalizing him."

"You should have their support." Since weeklong camps had started in the spring, he'd seen how stressed many of the parents were, how near to breaking.

"I have great friends and neighbors. I told you," she said firmly. "No pity party."

"Fair enough," he conceded.

She stared down into her cobbler, the silence stretching out between them. Finally she looked up. She stirred a spoon through the ice cream on the side. "Do you always deliver dessert to the campers?"

The question hung in the air between them, loaded with a deeper meaning he couldn't answer. Sure, he was here for his grandmother, but he would have been here anyway.

He settled for answering honestly. "You're the first."

"Oh." The lone syllable came out breathy, the wind lifting her hair.

He reached to catch a lock, testing the fine red threads between his fingers before stroking it behind her ear. Her eyes went wide, wary, but with a spark of interest he couldn't miss. For a long moment that stretched, loaded with temptation and want, he considered kissing her. Just leaning in and placing his mouth over hers to see if the chemistry between them was as explosive as he expected.

But that wariness in her eyes held him back. He had limited time with her. One mistaken move and he wouldn't have the chance to make it right before she left.

He angled back, pushing to his feet. "I should let you turn in. Morning comes early here."

She blinked fast, standing. "Thank you for the dessert." She stacked the containers and backed toward the door with them clutched in a white-knuckled grip. "I assume I will see you tomorrow?"

"You most definitely will."

It was only dessert. Only a touch to her hair.

And just that fast, she was tied up in knots over a man she'd met this morning. A cowboy.

God, she felt like a cliché.

Nina stood at the sink and scraped the last bite of gooey dessert down the disposal before tossing the disposable container in the trash. And God, it would be so easy to stand here at the sink and watch Alex through the window as he walked away. She'd only known him for a day. She wished she could just call it physical attraction, but she'd enjoyed talking to him. Even liked the way he could let peace settle for moments, as well.

Maybe she was simply starved for adult interaction. Her only time with other grown-ups centered on Cody's doctors' appointments or therapies. Even his play group focused on children with special needs. She wanted to give Cody every opportunity possible. But she couldn't deny her life was lonely no matter what she'd told Alex about having friends back home. The only interaction she had with others was volunteering in Cody's preschool program. Some said she should use that time for herself, and she tried. But it was easier said than done.

This week truly was a relaxing gift for her and Cody. She dropped onto the fluffy fat sofa. The cabin was cozy, comfy. A pink and green quilt—Texas two-step pattern on a brass bed. The whole place was an advertisement for Lone Star relaxation without being hokey. A colorful rag rug was soft under her feet. The lantern-style lamps and overhead light were made to resemble a flicker flame.

She should really finish unpacking and get some sleep.

Her well-traveled luggage rested on a pinewood bench. But her mind kept swirling with all the dreams she'd once stored in that case. She'd taken that suitcase with her to college, then New York City. The stickers all over the vintage piece advertised countries she'd dreamed of visiting. Warren had bought her a new set after they married, but she couldn't bring herself to throw the old ones out. After her divorce, she'd donated the honeymoon designer luggage to charity and reclaimed her old "dreams for the future" set. Those changes had felt like a reclaiming of her values and hopes.

Her cell phone chimed, interrupting her swirling thoughts. She leaned from the sofa to grab her purse off the coffee table. Her stomach leaped at the possibility that Alex might be calling. He had access to her number from her registration.

She glanced at the screen. Disappointment jabbed at her. Then guilt. She should be thankful her friend Reed was checking in on her. She and Reed had met at a play group for their children. A nice guy, a single father of a little girl with Down syndrome. His partner had left him over the stress of having a special-needs child. Nina understood the mark that betrayal left. They helped each other when they could, but they both had such very full plates.

"Hello, Reed." She propped her feet on the coffee table. "You're up late. Morning's going to come early for you getting Wendy to the bus stop."

Reed owned a bistro and took his daughter to work with him when she wasn't in school. Little Wendy loved the activity and charmed the customers.

"I'm not the only one up late," her friend teased back, his Northern accent so different from a particular cowboy drawl. "Did you lose your phone? I've been calling for a couple of hours. Just wanted to be sure you arrived safely."

"I was outside on the porch talking to…" She couldn't bring herself to tell him about Alex, not that there was much to tell. So she fibbed. "I was talking with another parent. Cody was asleep. The nights here are…idyllic."

"How did Cody enjoy his day?"

She grasped the safer topic with both hands. "He was enthralled by everything here. We're only a day into it, but I'm cautiously optimistic we're going to make a breakthrough here."

"I wish I could be there to see that."

"You have a restaurant to run."

"True enough. So tell me more about the camp."

What parts should she share with him? That she suddenly understood about the cowboy appeal? Or at least the appeal of one cowboy in particular? Reed was a friend, but not the kind of friend to whom she could say anything like that. "I was nervous coming up here that the camp would just be some overpriced excuse for parents to get a break. But it really is all about the children."

"Such as?"

"They had pony rides but let the parents lead the children around so they would feel more at ease. The menu is kid-friendly with a variety of choices so even kids with issues about texture will find something that works." And the adult fare was delicious, especially when delivered by a hot man who looked at her with hungry eyes. She hadn't felt like a desirable woman in so very long.

"That's awesome, really awesome. I'm glad you're getting this break and able to spend time with other adults. You spend too much time alone cooped up in your house."

True enough, but she didn't want to dwell on negative thoughts. She sagged to sit on the edge of the brass bed. "You must have called for a reason…"

"Can't I just check on you because you should have people looking out for you?"

"Sure you can, but I also hear something in your voice that worries me." She traced the pink and green pattern on the quilt.

"Your mother-in-law called. She'd gone by your town house and realized you'd left. She checked again this evening."

"What did you tell her?" Her mother-in-law didn't approve of her choice to keep Cody at home, and Nina knew she would just get blowback for choosing this camp. Her mother-in-law would come up with a million reasons why it was wrong.

"I said you went on a weeklong vacation with Cody. She wanted to know where. I told her to call you if she wanted details."

"Thank you." Sighing, she sagged back onto the bed, her head sinking into the pillows. "I appreciate that."

"Stop worrying. They're not going to get custody of Cody. There's no reason for a judge to pass over custody to them."

"Thank you again. I feel like I'm saying that all the time, but I mean it." She stared up at the ceiling fan slicing lazy shadows across the room, the distant echo of a band playing at the lodge penetrated the walls like a soft lullaby. "They just want to lock him away and control his inheritance. They don't love him. Not really."

"I know. And so will any judge who looks at the facts. When my partner tried to get out of helping with child support, my lawyer was on me 24/7 to keep a journal," Reed said with the unerring persistence that made him a force to be reckoned with in the courtroom. "Write a detailed accounting of your schedule and outings. Document. Document. Document. You'll have the facts on your side."

"Aye-aye, sir," she teased. "I will. Now you should stop worrying and get some sleep."

"You too. And be sure to take lots of photos of Cody."

"I will. And give little Wendy a hug from me. Tell her I'll bring her a present."

"Sure will," he said, an unmistakable affection leaking into his voice. He loved his daughter. "I'll be checking for text message photos."

"You're a good friend." And such a good man. They could have a great life together—except for the fact that they weren't attracted to each other. At all. Not a chance ever, since she wasn't a guy. "Good night, and thanks."

She disconnected the call, the taste of blueberries and the tangy scent of a certain cowboy's soap still teasing her senses.

God, on the one hand she had an amazing friend she could never sleep with. On the other hand she had a week with the hottest man she'd ever met. Too bad she'd never been the fling sort. But with the memory of Alex's touch still buzzing through her, she wondered if maybe she could be.

Three

Alex propped his boots on the office desk, the morning routine stable noises wrapping around him. Except today he couldn't get into the groove. Thoughts of Nina Lowery had him tied up into hitch knots.

He'd spent most of the night on the porch in a hammock, staring up at the stars, trying to reconcile his blaring conscience with his shouting libido. By sun-up, he'd reconciled himself to the fact that he couldn't hide his identity indefinitely. He would tell her who he was today and take it from there. It wasn't as if he'd actively tried to pry those stocks from her hands, and she had no reason to expect he would.

And he was genuinely interested in her.

What did he intend to do with this relentless attraction? It would be so much simpler if they'd just met somewhere outside the Hidden Gem Ranch. Not that he left this patch of earth often.

He cranked back in his chair, peering out in the open barn area that was more like a stadium, used for parties. The kids had worn themselves out with a morning of nature walks and a wagon ride picnic. Now they were napping in the cool barn on mats, a wide-screen television showing a video for the spare few who hadn't fallen asleep.

He scanned the familiar walls of home. Like in all their stables and barns, custom saddles lined the corridors, all works of art like everything the McNairs made. Carvings marked the leather with a variety of designs from roses to vines to full-out scenes. Some saddles sported silver or brass studs on horn caps and skirting edges rivaling the tooling of the best old vaqueros. He'd explored every inch of this place, starting when he was younger than those kids sleeping out there.

And speaking of those snoozing kids…

This would be a good time to clear up his identity issues. That much he could do—and should do—before making any other decisions about Nina.

He shoved up from his desk and walked down the hall, angling past a table of drying art projects made of leaves used for papier-mâché. Nina sat beside her son, cross-legged on the floor with a reading tablet in her hand.

Snagging a bottle of water off the snack table, Alex made his way over to her. He sidestepped sleeping children. Every step of the way he enjoyed the opportunity to look at her. Her hair was swept up on top of her head, a couple of red spirals brushed her forehead and one trailed down her neck. His hands itched to test the feel of her hair between his fingers, to tug one of those locks and let it spring back. What was she reading?

He wanted to know that as much as he wanted to touch her hair again, and this time run his fingers through the wavy curls.

Alex squatted down next to her, extending the water. "You need to stay hydrated."

She glanced up from her tablet, her eyes flickering with surprise, then happiness. She was glad to see him.

"Thank you." She set aside her book and tugged open her canvas bag to reveal three bottles of spring water. "But I'm set for *agua*."

He twisted the top of his bottle for himself. "What are you reading?"

"*Madame Bovary*."

"In French?" He thought of her speaking multiple languages.

She tapped her temple. "Keeping my skills sharp."

Cody stirred on his nap mat.

Alex froze, waited until the boy settled back into sleep with a drowsy sigh. Hesitating for a moment, Nina rose carefully. Alex gestured toward the door, tipping his head to the side in question. She tucked away her tablet and pulled out a bottle of water. Why did he feel as if he'd just won the grand prize? She followed him to the open barn doors, the wind sweeping inside as the low drone of the movie filled the air.

She lifted her drink and tapped his in a toast. "I truly do appreciate the thought even though I brought my own."

"You're a planner." As was he. He liked the regimentation needed to run this place, enjoyed the challenge.

"I wasn't always, but I have to be now." She gazed back into the barn at her son with obvious love and protectiveness in her eyes. "My son depends on me."

There was a strain in the corner of her eyes. He wanted to brush his thumbs along her cheeks until she rested. "I'm sorry you don't have more family to help out. Family is...everything."

As if he needed a reminder of the stakes for him here.

An awkward silence settled.

He'd met a woman he wanted to be with and her family posed a threat to his way of life. If she even would have him in the first place. She seemed attracted, but wary as hell—with reason.

An older cowboy brushed past, clapping Alex on the shoulder. "Hey, boss, mind if I take the afternoon off to go to my daughter's spelling bee?"

Alex waved. "Enjoy. I've got this under control."

"Great. My wife will have my hide if I don't make this, and I gotta confess, I would have been there anyway." The older cowboy's smile spread. "I'll pull overtime tomorrow."

"No thanks needed. Just tell the little genius good luck from Uncle Alex."

"Can do, boss."

Alex winced at the last word. Boss. So much for telling her on his own terms. He hung his head, wondering how she would react to his identity being revealed. Hell, he should have told her last night. Or even fifteen minutes ago.

Turning slowly, he prepared himself, surprised at the disappointment churning in his gut. He couldn't blame his grandmother either. This was his own fault... Except he didn't find anger in Nina's eyes.

Just curiosity. "You said you wanted to talk?"

Apparently she'd written off the "boss" comment to him being a foreman of some sort. He had to clear this up or it was going to explode in his face. "Let's go somewhere quieter."

Away from people who would tell her too much before he was ready for her to know. He guided her into the warm sunshine.

"Um, sure." She looked around nervously. "But I need to keep Cody in sight."

"Of course." He took her hand and tugged her toward a corral a few yards away, the only spot with a clear line of sight to the barn but also out of the hustle and bustle of ranch workers and guests.

She looked around, leaning back on a split-rail fence. "What's all the activity outside about? Seems like more than regular work and tourists."

"We host major events around here, parties, rehearsal dinners and weddings." The last word made him wince. One wedding in particular.

"Even in the middle of the camp going on?"

"Even then. We have a lot of land, more than just this one space, and we intend to keep it that way." Which reminded him of his grandmother's test as well as the Lowerys and their plans to convert the place into some Wild West theme park. "We pride ourselves on people feeling their event is private."

She angled her head to the side, her high-swept ponytail swishing. "And which event are they working on now?"

"A large-scale rehearsal dinner and wedding, actually." His cousin's wedding to Johanna. Alex was over any feelings for her, but he wanted the damn awkwardness to go away. "I bet your city-girl imagination is running wild at the notion of a country wedding."

The corners of her lips twitched. "Are you accusing me of thinking in clichés?"

"If the square dance fits." He winked.

She laughed, the melody of the sound filling the space between them and filling him up, making him want to haul her close. He needed more time with her. He just had to figure out how to balance his grandmother's request with his wish to be with the woman all week, no interference muddying the waters.

"Nina," he said, hooking a boot on the rail as he leaned back beside her, "there are all sorts of things going on at this place, including events planned for the camp parents."

She looked at him through her long eyelashes. "I read every word of the brochures and registration literature."

He allowed himself the luxury of tugging a curl, testing the softness between her fingers. "You're not interested in a spa treatment while your son naps? Or a sitter after he goes to sleep?"

Her eyes fluttered closed briefly and then steadied, staying open. "I'm here for Cody. Not for myself. I can't just turn off that mom switch."

He got that. And he sure as hell didn't expect her to neglect her son. He understood how it felt to be a kid shuffled to the side. "What about riding lessons?"

Confusion shifted across her face. "Excuse me?"

"If you want to be a part of your son's world, how about experience it firsthand? Cody's sleeping and the stable is next door." He set aside their half-drunk water bottles on the split-rail fence and called to one of their gentlest mares. A pudgy, warm chocolate–colored horse walked toward them with slow, ambling steps. And sure, Alex knew he was delaying his real purpose for speaking with her today, but he couldn't resist enjoying what could be his last chance to spend more time with her. "Consider becoming acquainted with one of our horses?"

She looked at the horse and tucked her arms behind her back, shaking her head. "No, thank you. I don't think so."

He hadn't considered that even as a city girl she might not like the ranch. "Are you afraid of horses?"

"Not afraid so much as…uncertain," she said hesitantly, holding up her hands. "My son is fascinated, so I'm here for him, but I can't say I share his fascination."

He didn't sense a dislike of horses. Just nerves and lack of knowledge. The notion of introducing her stirred him. "We all have preferences. Even if you're not an equestrian fan, I can see you want to know more about your son's world. So for his sake, give this a try." He raised his hands and linked fingers with hers, wondering why he wasn't telling her about who he was. Instead he was touching her, watching the flicker of the sun in her green eyes, and he couldn't bring himself to change course, not just yet. "We can take it slow?"

Her throat moved in a gulp. "Meaning what?"

"Just get to know Amber." He guided her hand along the mare's neck, Nina's soft skin making him ache to touch more of her. "Check out the feel of her. She's a gentle sweetheart."

Gasping, Nina stroked the horse again, reverently almost. "Wow, I didn't know. I rode a little as a child, but I only remember how scared I was and how bad it hurt to fall off. I thought she would feel bristly, but her coat is like satin."

"You've truly never been around a horse before?"

And yet she'd come here for her son, even though the horse clearly scared her every bit as much as she entranced her.

"I can feel her heartbeat." Her awe and laughter stoked him.

He kept his hand over hers, his eyes locked on her gaze, watching her entranced by the animal. "She can hear yours."

Nina turned and met his gaze. She wanted him. He could see that clearly, felt her desire crackling off her skin and into him.

Unable to resist, he dipped his head and kissed her. Just a simple kiss because they were outside and anyone could walk up to them. But damn it, this was his last chance before he would have to tell her about his grandmother's plan, and then he didn't know if he would get another opportunity. The thought of never tasting her, never knowing the feel of her was more than he could wrap his brain around.

She tasted like fresh spring water and the fruit salad from lunch. Strawberries and grapes. His hands curled around her shoulders. Soft. Warm. Such a perfect fit. Sparks shot through him, damn near knocking him senseless, as if he'd been tossed from a horse onto his head.

God, how he wanted to haul her closer, but they were out here in the open. A good thing, actually, because he still needed to talk to her. He couldn't go further. In fact, he had already taken more than he'd planned. But damn, she was tempting. And if she booted him on his ass once she found out who he was, what would he do?

The sound of a little boy's screams split the air.

Nina's supple body went rigid in his arms.

"Cody," she gasped against his mouth, pulling back. "My son. That's my son."

Frantic, repetitive screeches grew louder by the second. Nina tore out of Alex's arms and raced back to the barn.

Nina bit down the well of nausea born of pure panic. The smell of hay and dust threatened to choke her with each breath. Instead of making out with a man she'd only met yesterday, she should have been watching her son. She searched the barn, following the noise and finding her son on the far side, in a line of children waiting outside the bathroom.

Relief almost buckled her knees. He was fine. Safe.

But he was definitely having a meltdown. He needed her and she wasn't there with him. Her fault. Irresponsible. And just the sort of thing her in-laws would be watching for to claim their right to have custody of her son.

What if they had one of their private detectives here watching her now? She'd tried to keep this trip quiet, but her in-laws were cunning.

Alex raced past her, his boots pounding the earthen floor of the barn, past the now-blank movie screen, to the line of children.

He knelt in front of Cody, not touching. "What's wrong, sport?"

Her son stomped his feet, faster and faster, crying. Two camp counselors backed away, giving Cody space and looking at her with a shrug.

She resisted the urge to rush forward. Startling movements could upset Cody again, and focusing on Alex seemed to be calming him for now.

"Not his turn," Cody insisted.

Alex angled closer, not touching but using the breadth of his shoulders to block out the rest of the world and reduce distractions. "Excuse me?"

Without looking up, her son pointed at a boy wearing braces on his legs. "Not his turn," Cody gasped, tears streaking down his blotchy face. "He cut the line."

Nina stepped up and whispered, "He's comforted by rules and order."

The camp counselor, a slim blonde woman, was already sliding in to restore order, gently and ably distracting the child who'd innocently pushed to the front of the line. Or maybe not innocently. Children were children regardless of disabilities or special needs. But Nina was beginning to see that these counselors truly had the skills to manage the special issues these children faced.

"Cody," the camp counselor said softly but firmly, "breathe with me. Deep breaths at the same time I do."

And within a couple of dozen slow exhales, Nina's son was back under control again. Crisis averted for now. In fact, looking back, the meltdown hadn't been one of his worst. The teacher had read the signs and acted.

Nina knelt beside the camp counselor. "Thank you so much." Then she glanced at Alex. "And thank you for reaching him so quickly."

She forced herself to meet his gaze, tougher than she would have expected from just a half-innocent brush of their lips. But there had been so much more in the moment than she could remember feeling…ever. Though she didn't have a lot of first kisses in her life, this one ranked up there as the very best.

And the most unexpected.

One she ached to have happen again. Soon. But not with her son around. God, she was a mess.

She drew in a deep breath for herself this time. "I should take Cody back to our cabin for a while." She stepped away, slowly. "Thank you for introducing me to the horse—Amber—and for the help with my little guy."

"My pleasure." His hand cupped her shoulder, re-igniting the sparks in her belly. "After your son falls asleep, would you mind if I stopped by again?"

What? Did he actually expect they would jump in bed together because of a simple kiss? Okay, not such a simple kiss. A brief kiss that packed more of a wal-lop than most full make-out sessions.

Did he use this camp as a pickup pool full of easy marks, needy, lonely moms? But how could she ask as much with so many people around them?

"Alex, I don't think seeing each other tonight is such a good idea."

"With dessert," he said carefully. "Truth. Nothing more than dessert, and I never got to tell you what I planned when we walked outside."

"Tell me now," she pressed, even though the thought of having him come to her cabin tonight was damn tempting.

He hesitated and there was something in his blue eyes she couldn't read. "It's too noisy here. Cody's still on edge…this isn't the time."

"Okay, but just dessert. Nothing more," she said care-fully. Curious. Nervous. And yes, she wanted to see Alex again at a time when she could be sure her son was 100 percent safe and settled, because the times for her to be a woman were few and far between.

He touched the brim on his hat. "Nothing more... unless you say otherwise."

Alex tucked out of the kitchen, through the back door of the family's private quarters, carrying a container with two fat slices of chocolate-raspberry cake. He really needed to up his game if he expected her to forgive him for holding back on who he was—and if he wanted a chance in hell of a repeat of the kiss earlier. A kiss that had rocked him back on his boot heels.

Except he had no clue what tack to take with her, and he couldn't figure that out until he got to know her better. If she gave him that chance after tonight. And then there was the whole issue with his grandmother and the stocks...

Hell, this better be some damn good chocolate-raspberry cake.

He stepped out onto the back lanai, lit with brass torches to keep the Texas-sized mosquitoes at bay. He stopped short at the sight of Amie, Stone and Stone's fiancée, Johanna, all having a dessert gathering of their own. Any other time he would have been fine sitting with them. He would have welcomed the chance to smooth the waters, to prove he was genuinely okay with Stone and Johanna as a couple. They were meant to be together. He got that. Nothing he'd ever felt for Johanna came close to the intense emotion coming from his normally reserved cousin.

Amie waved her fork in the air. "Join us," the former beauty pageant queen said. "We've been waiting for you."

A family ambush? Great. "I'm on my way out for the evening. Rain check."

His stubborn twin just smiled and shook her head, her long black ponytail draped over one shoulder. "It can wait." Amie leaned to pull out a chair for him, a gray tabby cat leaping from her lap. "We need to talk."

He considered telling her no—not enough people told Amie no—but whatever she needed to say might have something to do with their grandmother.

Or God forbid, the upcoming wedding.

He set his container full of cake on the tiled table. "Make it quick. I really do have somewhere to be in fifteen minutes."

Stone had an arm draped over his fiancée's chair. "I heard Gran called you in for a special meeting yesterday."

Word traveled fast around here. How much did they know? Not much if they were ganging up on him this way.

"We just had lunch." The last thing he wanted were the details of his "test" going public. That wouldn't be fair to Nina.

"How did Gran look?" Johanna leaned forward, her fingers toying with the diamond horseshoe necklace Mariah had given her. "She went to the doctor today and it wore her out so much she wasn't taking visitors."

Alarm twisted the knot in his gut tighter. "She looked tired. But determined."

The tabby cat bounded off the lanai and Johanna shoved up from her chair to race after it, even though it was Amie's pet—a part of their ongoing battle about indoor vs. outdoor cats.

"So?" Amie licked her fork clean. "What did you and Gram talk about?"

Alex leaned back in his chair, arms crossed over her chest. "Why are you making such a production out of me having lunch with my terminally ill grandmother?"

Amie chewed her bottom lip. "We used to be able to talk about anything. We're twins."

Stone studied Alex through narrowed eyes and said softly, "Are you ditching us because of the wedding?"

Leave it to Stone to throw it out there. At least Johanna was still chasing the cat through the shrubbery. "I've made it clear I'm happy for both of you, and I mean that." Might as well go for broke. "In fact, I'm asking a new friend to come with me to the wedding."

"Who?"

"You don't know her." And Lord, he hoped Nina was still talking to him after tonight. He brushed his thumb along the top of the boxed dessert, his memory filling with that world-rocking kiss.

Stone relaxed back in his seat. "That's good to know. You're just so damn quiet it's tough to get a read off you, and we're all on edge with the new CEO stepping in and Gran's—"

Amie sat up bolt. "Gran gave you your test, didn't she?"

His twin always had been able to read his mind. Most of the time he could see right through her as well, but she had up walls today. He should have noticed before, but he'd been so wrapped up in himself. Damn it. "Amie—"

She stabbed her fork in the cake. "I knew it!" She clapped her hands. "My life is boring as hell these days, so spill. What's your test?"

Nuh-uh. His secret for now. He shoved out of his seat and grabbed the boxed dessert. "If you want to know, ask her. But I suspect if she wanted you two to know, she would have invited you to lunch." He stepped away, determined to share as much as he could with Nina to lessen the chance of this blowing up in his face. "Now if you'll excuse me, I have a date and I'm running late."

He was ten minutes late.

Gripping the arms of the porch rocker, Nina told herself it shouldn't matter. She didn't care. But she did. She'd spent the past hour since her son went to bed showering and changing into white shorts and a silky shirt that showed off her arms and legs. She'd put on makeup and dried her hair out, straightening the curls. All because of one kiss from a guy she would only see for a week.

And then?

What would life be like when she returned to San Antonio with nothing but memories? The thought chilled her.

She shot to her feet and yanked open the front door to go back inside. She refused to appear overeager—or heaven forbid—desperate.

Still, at the sound of his footsteps on her porch steps, her stomach lurched. Damn it. Pressing a hand against her butterfly-filled stomach, she realized she had to regain control. For starters, she had to be honest with herself.

Yes, she was attracted to him. Very. And clearly he was attracted to her too. She hadn't misread that. Plus, he was so different from her silver-spoon-born ex. Alex was down-to-earth, a regular kind of guy.

And he was knocking on her door.

Late.

She yanked a scrunchie off the table and pulled her hair back into a ponytail. If anything happened here, she needed to be back in control—and never let him know he'd rattled her.

She grabbed a magazine for good measure and folded it open as if she'd been casually reading before she opened the door.

Her stomach flipped again.

She stepped outside, a much safer place to be with this man who tempted her.

She took the dessert box from him and sat in the porch rocker, only to realize the pitcher of lemonade she'd prepared earlier gave away how eager she'd been to see him. She was revealing too much of herself too fast. It was time to level the playing field.

"Alex, what did you come to tell me?"

He blinked in surprise. "You sure do cut right to the chase."

"The sooner you tell me, the sooner I can have my dessert." She tried to add levity even as nerves tap danced in her stomach. Did he have to look so hot in jeans and a simple T-shirt, his Stetson resting on his knee?

"I think we've had some miscommunication." His work calloused fingers drummed along the brim of his hat. "And I don't want you to think I misled you."

An option she'd never considered broadsided her, sending a flush of mortification, anger and disappointment through her. "Oh my God. You're married." Her breath hitched as she gasped, inhaling faster and faster. She pressed her hands to her face. "I should have thought to ask. But you're not wearing a ring, and yes, I looked—"

His hand clamped around her wrist. "No, I'm not married." He pulled her hands down and held them in his. "Hell no, actually. Never have been."

"Oh." She laughed nervously, hyperaware of her hands clasped in his. "Are you trying to tell me you're involved with someone else—"

"I'm not with another woman."

Relief flooded her, so much she wanted to launch herself at him for another kiss, one much deeper than the public one earlier. A kiss where she wrapped her arms and body around him, feeling the hard planes of those muscles against her. *Oh. My.*

She needed to rein herself in and find out what he wanted to tell her first. "Not that it matters, since we just met and this isn't anything like…or…um…"

"And before you ask," he said deliberately, shoving aside the table between them and leaning in closer to her, "I'm straight."

His knee brushed hers, the warm denim against her bare skin setting her senses on fire. He'd angled so close she could see the peppering of his late-day beard and her fingers itched to explore the raspy terrain, get to know the masculine feel of him.

She clenched her fingers against temptation. "I wasn't saying… Um, I wasn't… Oh hell. It's okay by me if you're—"

He leaned in closer, his clear blue eyes holding her. "I'm one hundred percent straight and one hundred percent attracted to you."

The night air went hot and humid fast, heavy with innuendo and need. She wanted him. Her body was shouting that truth at her. She wanted to have a wild and passionate fling with this man. No complications. A simple cowboy she would only know this week. A man who was the total opposite of her privileged, spoiled ex-husband. A man she would say farewell to in a week and who could give her sweet memories to carry with her.

She squeezed his hands and said, "Okay, that's nice to know. Very nice."

"And that's why I need to clear something up before you hear from someone else. I'm not a hired hand at the ranch. I'm a McNair. My family owns the place."

Four

Alex's revelation stunned Nina silent. She snatched her hands from his.

Songs of deep-throated bullfrogs filled the quiet void as she clutched the arms of her porch rocker. Of all the things she'd expected to hear from Alex, this was last on the list. In her experience in New York City and with her ex's family, millionaire bosses didn't run around in dusty jeans.

Betrayal bit like persistent mosquitoes. The sting lingered, itching even as she told herself it shouldn't matter. She thought back, though, and all the signs were there. She'd even heard him called "boss" and let herself hear what she'd wanted. She'd heard of the McNair family but didn't keep track of all their first names.

But the heir? The McNair who oversaw the Hidden Gem Lodge? He wasn't a regular, easygoing cowboy.

And he was now the last sort of man she could consider for a fling. "You're serious? Your family owns the Hidden Gem Ranch?"

"As well as Diamonds in the Rough Jewelers. Yes, my cousins and I have run the family empire together. The Hidden Gem is my domain."

"And the rest of holdings?"

"My cousin Stone was the CEO of Diamonds in the Rough before he founded the camp. My twin sister, Amie, works for the company as a designer. We all own a portion of the portfolio, but our grandmother is the major stockholder."

Squeezing her eyes closed, she let his words sink in. Had she been dense about the "boss" part on purpose because she didn't want to know the truth or had she just been so dazzled by this man she couldn't think straight?

Hook, line and sinker, she'd bought in to the whole cowboy fantasy. Except the fantasy wasn't true at all. Alex was a rich businessman just like her ex. She scratched her arms along those imagined stings. She should go inside and close the door on him and her feelings.

Instead she opened her eyes and asked him, "Why did you mislead me?"

Remorse chased through his eyes, at least she thought it did. She wasn't sure who or what to trust right now, not even herself.

He rested his hand carefully on her wrist, squeezing lightly when she didn't pull away. "You didn't recognize me and it's rare I get to hang out with someone who thinks of me like a regular Joe Shmoe. I like to think I'm a good judge of character, but there are still people out there who only see the money."

His explanation made sense. She wanted to buy in to it and believe she could indulge in a harmless flirtation this week—maybe more. Still, the oversight rankled. "I hear what you're saying, but it still doesn't seem right."

"Does that mean you're not open to more dessert together?" he asked with a slow drawl and a half smile.

Goose bumps rose along her skin, the good kind. Could she just go with the flow here? It wasn't as if he'd claimed to be rich when he wasn't just to impress someone, and she wasn't committing to anything long-term.

"Okay," she conceded. "Since you came clean so quickly, I think I can overlook your allowing me to get the wrong idea about you. If you'd kept the truth from me for weeks or months that would be a different matter."

"Glad to know we've cleared that up."

She eased her wrist away and considered her words carefully, honestly. "To be honest, if you'd spilled the whole 'I'm a McNair' at the start, I probably would have thought you were bragging or feeling entitled."

He shuddered in mock horror. "My grandmother would absolutely not allow that."

She studied him through narrowed eyes, trying to reconcile this new piece of information about him. "You're really not a ranch hand or a foreman? You looked like such a natural."

"I'm a hands-on kind of boss." He clapped a hand to his chest. "And I'm getting the vibe that the boss issue is a problem for you."

"I'm just...unsettled." Her rocking chair squeaked against the wooden porch floor.

He leaned forward, elbows on his knees working his

hat between his hands. "It's nice to have someone to speak with who isn't caught up in the McNair portfolio."

"Sure…"

"But you're still uncomfortable."

"I'm adjusting. You live over there—" she pointed to the mansion lodge "—and I'm more comfortable in a cottage." Although her son had an inheritance that entitled him to so much more. But until she knew what the future held for Cody, she needed to be all the more cautious with his investments in case he couldn't ever work to support himself.

"Yes, I live in the family's half of the lodge. It's sectioned off into private suites." He set his hat on the table and took her hand back again, holding tighter this time. "But that's just brick and mortar, logs and rocks. It's not who we are."

"And who are you, Alex McNair?" she asked, because the image of him as a coddled rich kid didn't fit what she was seeing in him and his hands-on attitude. However, she knew how well a person could hide his real nature. "Why did you feel the need to let me misunderstand your role here for two days?"

He linked their fingers, his eyes glinting in the moonlight. "Meet me for dinner tomorrow night and let's find out about each other."

"My son is here for camp. I'm here for him, not for…" She stumbled on the word and held up their linked hands. "For whatever this is you think we might do this week."

But hadn't she just been considering a fling? Still, she needed it to be her decision, and this wasn't the kind of impulsive choice she'd ever made before.

"You're interested too. We're both adults. What's

wrong with us enjoying each other's company for the week you'll be here?"

Company? Could he mean that word as innocently as it sounded, or was there a hidden innuendo? "Do you see this program as a way to pick up vulnerable women short-term, no strings, and you get to say goodbye at the end of a weeklong camp?"

"Whoa." His eyebrows shot up in shock. "That's a lot to unpack in one sentence. I'll opt for a quick answer, 'no.'"

"No, what?" she asked suspiciously.

"No, I do not make a practice of picking up any kind of vacationer coming to the Hidden Gem. In fact, this is very atypical of me." He rubbed the inside of her wrist with his thumb. "And the last thing I would call you is vulnerable. You come off as a strong woman in charge of her life."

She rolled her eyes. "Flattery. But thanks."

"You're welcome. So, are we having dinner together tomorrow or not? After Cody's asleep of course, and under the care of one of our certified child care providers. There's a dinner boat cruise that's nice, public. No pressure."

He made the offer sound so easy. "I'll think about it."

"Fair enough." His stroke shifted from her wrist to her sensitive palm. "I'll stop by at lunch tomorrow to get your answer."

"At lunch?" She wasn't even sure what she was saying; her brain scrambled at the touch that was somehow so very intimate without being overt. What a time to realize how very little human contact she had in her life anymore.

"I happen to have gotten a sneak peek at the itinerary

from a very reliable source, and the kids are roasting hot dogs for lunch tomorrow at eleven. By noon they'll be in a saddle polishing class. Meet me while your son is settled under the attentive eye of the instructors and we can talk."

"I can't promise he'll let me leave," she said, wanting to turn the tables on him but not sure how yet. "I don't want to risk another meltdown."

"Understood. I can be flexible."

She stared at him with suspicion, chewing her bottom lip.

"What?" Alex asked.

She gave up and blurted, "You're too good to be true. It must be an act."

"Aw, Nina." His hand slid up to cup her face. "People can be genuine."

She couldn't help being enticed by the promise in his eyes. Yet pain from past betrayals welled up over how her husband and her in-laws had so deeply let her down. Worse, how they had let down precious Cody. "They can be. But they usually aren't."

He stroked back her hair, tucking it behind her ear. "Then why are you even considering having dinner with me?"

"I honestly don't know." Her scalp tingled from the light brush of his fingers, his nearness overriding boundaries she thought were firmly in place.

Their gazes met, eyes held. She breathed him in, remembering the feel of his lips on hers.

Would he kiss her again? Because if he did, she wasn't sure she could say no to anything. Her body was on fire from just having him near and a few simple caresses. He angled forward and her heart tripped over itself for a couple of beats.

He passed the dessert box over. "Chocolate-raspberry cake. Enjoy."

His lips skimmed her forehead so briefly, so softly, her breath hitched and then he was gone, jogging down the cabin steps and disappearing in the tree line.

Drawing in a steadying breath, she released it on a shuddering sigh.

No doubt about it, she had a serious willpower problem when it came to this particular cowboy.

The next day at lunchtime, Alex angled through the different stations of children enjoying camp activities from saddle polishing to panning for gold in a sandbox to using hula hoops for lassoing wooden horses. His cousin Stone had told him the activities helped with motor skills and confidence. Cody looked more relaxed today as he worked on cleaning the little saddle resting on stacked bales of hay. Nina sat on a bale beside her child, the sunshine highlighting streaks of gold in her red curls.

He was still pumped over how well the conversation had gone the night before. He'd learned a lot about her, more than she might have intended to let on. She was a wary woman and someone had obviously hurt her in the past, most likely her ex-husband. That would be important to keep in mind if Alex wanted a chance with her. He needed to tread smartly.

Nina Lowery was a tactile woman. He'd gauged her responses carefully, watching her pupils widen with arousal as he'd stroked her wrist, then massaged her palm. Her senses were hungry and he intended to feed them.

Even now her fingers were testing the texture of everything around, flitting from the bale of hay to the stirrups on the saddle.

She hadn't booted him out on his butt. She'd actually given him another chance. He was skating on thin ice with those stocks in play. It wasn't as if they were entering into some long-term relationship. She made it clear she was leaving in a week and her son filled her life.

Knowing that made him want to pamper her all the more while she was here.

Alex stopped behind Nina, resting a hand on her shoulder. "Good afternoon, beautiful."

She shivered under his hand. But in a good way.

He let his touch linger for a second before he stepped over to Cody. "You're doing a great job there, cowboy."

"Make it smooth," he said, stroking.

The instructor, a special ed teacher from a local school who'd been glad for the extra income working at the camp, stepped closer. "Cody's doing a fantastic job. I think he's having fun."

The boy nodded, his hands circling repetitive strokes over the leather, cowboy hat perched on his blond head and protecting him from the sun. "Having fun."

Nina pressed her hand to her chest, emotions obvious in her expressive eyes. "I knew this was a good idea, but I had no clue how amazing equine-assisted learning could be for my son, for all these children."

"I'm glad to hear that. My cousin worked hard searching for professionals to employ. It's important to do this right."

"Well, he succeeded." Nina smiled over her shoulder

at him. "I'm impressed with the way they've combined physical and speech therapy. And they've blended balance, posture, hand-to-eye coordination and communication skills into activities that are fun, making it seem more like play."

He hadn't thought about it that way before, but it made sense. "Horses are herd animals. They seek connections and have a way of communicating, a bond, that goes beyond words."

"I can see that." Her gaze shifted back to her child. "Most of all, I appreciate the self-confidence and self-esteem Cody's finding in these classes in such a short time. It's impressive how the different stations are geared for each child's special need. They've approached Cody with sensory activities, without overloading him." She glanced back at Alex. "But that's not what you came for. Yes."

"What?" he asked, having lost track of the conversation. He was locked in on the sound of her voice and the berry scent of her shampoo.

"Yes, I'll accompany you on the dinner cruise."

"Excellent." He folded his arms over his chest and rocked back on his boot heels.

She looked at him quickly. "You're staying?"

"This camp may be my cousin's endeavor, but it's a part of the McNair empire, happening on McNair lands. I care." He shrugged. "And it's my lunch break. I'd like to spend it with you. If that's okay?"

"Sure," she said, her eyes wide with surprise. "We could take a walk? The counselors encourage parents to step away today. You know that, since you've read the itinerary."

"Guilty as charged."

She laughed softly before kneeling to talk to her son, detailing where she was going and how long she would be gone, as well as what to do if he needed her. Cody nodded without looking away from his task.

"Cody," she said, "I need to know you understand."

He turned toward her and patted her shoulder with a clumsy thump, thump. "Bye, Mom."

Her smile at the simple connection stole the air from Alex's lungs. Then she stood, spreading her hands wide. "Lead the way."

Victory charged through his veins. He cupped her elbow and steered her around the different play stations, the controlled chaos of childish squeals all around them. "After yesterday's incident I thought you might be hesitant to go too far away."

"I feel more confident today than yesterday. So, would you like to show me around the place?"

"Actually, yes, I have something I believe you'll enjoy over by the pool area." He steered her along the path back to the main lodge, tree branches creating a shady canopy. "You'll still be able to see your son, but indulge yourself, as well."

"I don't have my swimsuit with me right now and a swim is on the schedule for later. I'll burn if I go twice."

"That's not what I mean." He gestured to the rustic canvas cabana off to the side of the pool area. "We're here for a couples' massage."

"What?" Her voice squeaked. No kidding, *squeaked*. Nina cleared her throat and tried again. "You must be joking."

"Not at all." He grinned wickedly. "My first choice was to fly you to my favorite restaurant for lunch, but

I knew that would be pushing my luck. So I opted for something here at the resort you would enjoy for an hour."

Horrified that she could have so misread him, she held up a palm and backed away. "We are *not* going to have massages together. God, I can't believe I trusted—"

"Wait." He grabbed her wrist, chuckling softly. "I'm not that clueless. Sorry for teasing you a bit there. If you pull back the curtain, you'll see it's just shoulder massages and a light lunch. Simple. No need to take off our clothes...unless you want, that is."

Her hand lowered. She'd been played, but in a funny way. She crinkled her nose. "You *are* a bad cowboy after all."

He held up his thumb and forefinger. "Just a bit."

Alex escorted her past the luxury pool area. One side of the tall stone fountain fed a waterfall into the shallow end of the pool. A hot tub bubbled invitingly on the other side of the fountain. Her in-laws were wealthy, but in a more steel-and-high-rise resort kind of way. Nina respected the way the McNairs had preserved the look of their place, even if it meant limiting customers. He stopped outside the cabana just as the curtain swept wide.

An older woman stepped out, frail, with short gray hair. Nina backed out of her way, but Alex urged her closer.

"Gran," he said, leaning in to give the older woman a kiss on the cheek.

So this was the indomitable Mariah McNair. The flyers about the camp had included the story of the senior McNairs' romance and how they'd built their dynasty.

Mariah had run the business side while her husband, Jasper, had been more of the artisan. The photo in the welcome packet bore only a passing resemblance to the woman in front of her, a woman whose health was clearly fading. Although her blue eyes were every bit as sharp and vibrant as her grandson's.

"Alex." Mariah smiled, looking frail but relaxed, a sheen of massage oils glinting on her neck. "Introduce me to this lovely lady."

Something flickered in Alex's eyes, but Nina couldn't quite figure out what. "Gran, this is Nina Lowery. Her son, Cody, is here for camp this week. Nina, this is my grandmother Mariah McNair."

The McNair matriarch extended a thin hand, veins spidery and blotched from what appeared to be multiple IVs. "It's a pleasure to meet you, dear. How is your child enjoying HorsePower?"

"Nice to meet you as well, Mrs. McNair." Nina shook the woman's cool hand and found the quick return clasp to be stronger than she would have expected. "My son is having a wonderful time, thank you. I'm amazed at how quickly the camp counselors have put him at ease."

"I'm glad to hear that." Mariah tucked her hands into the pockets of her loose jean jumper. "Leaving a positive legacy is important." She nodded to Nina. "Nice to meet you, dear. You'll have to pardon me, but I'm going to take a nap now." She waved to a younger woman behind her. Her nurse? An assistant?

Mariah walked slowly away, the other woman hovering close to catch her if she stumbled.

The pain in Alex's eyes was tangible.

Nina's parents had been older when she was born, so her memories of her grandparents were dim, but she recalled the grief of losing them, first to dementia, then to death. Nina touched his arm. "It's tough watching those we love grow older."

Alex rubbed the back of his neck. "She has cancer. Terminal."

"Oh no. Alex, I'm so very sorry."

He glanced over at her. "Me too. Nobody is ever okay with losing a loved one, but to be robbed of the years she should have had left is…just…" He rubbed the back of his neck hard. "Ah hell, I think I'm more than ready for that shoulder massage now."

And suddenly it was the most natural thing in the world to tuck her hand in the crook of his arm. "That sounds like an excellent idea. You'll have to pardon me if I'm antsy. I've never had a massage before. Lead the way."

He swept the canvas curtain aside, to reveal a massage table, two massage chairs and a team of massage therapists, just as he'd promised. The grandmotherly pair waited off to the side in simple black scrubs with the Hidden Gem logo on the pocket.

The canvas walls were lined with Aztec drapes. The music of Native American pipes drifted through the speakers and muffled sounds outside. Cooling fans swished overhead.

Nina eyed the massage chairs warily, designed for her to straddle, her back exposed and her face tucked into a doughnut-style cradle. Warily, she smiled at the therapists before sitting. The leather seat was cool, but the cover on the face cradle was cottony smooth with a hint of peppermint oils that opened her sinuses with each inhale.

Alex sat in the chair beside her, face in the cradle,

strong arms on the rests. Her view of him was limited, but then every bit of him intrigued her. It had been so long since she'd had a man in her life, the masculine details made her shivery all over. The dark hair sprinkled on his arms made her want to tease her fingers along his skin.

Clearing her throat, she shifted her eyes away from temptation. A tray of finger foods as well as glasses of green tea and lemon water with straws waited on a long table in front of them.

Never in a million years would she have expected him to come up with this idea. She heard the light rustle of footsteps as each masseuse took her place and whispered softly, "I'm going to start on your shoulders now. Let me know if you require more or less pressure."

At the first firm touch, Nina all but melted into the chair. Wow. Just wow. "Alex, this is…unexpected and incredible."

"Unexpected in what way?" His voice rumbled from beside her.

"That you thought of this and that you're here too, I guess," she answered, the last word turning to a low groan of pleasure. She reached for the lemon water and guided the straw through the face cradle for a sip. The scent of massage oils filled the air. Sage, perhaps?

"A good massage was crucial back in my rodeo days if I wanted to walk the next day. Even once my years on the circuit ended, I found I was still addicted."

She'd seen him on the wild horse that first day, but hadn't thought about his rodeo days. She turned her head enough to sneak a peek, her eyes roving over his body, envisioning those strong thighs gripping resistant bulls. She also thought of the kinds of falls he must have taken. He'd mentioned broken bones and she couldn't hide a wince at the pain he'd felt. She noticed a tiny scar peeking out of his hairline along his temple. Had he gotten that from a bad spill?

The masseuse gently guided her face back into the padded cradle of the chair and kneaded the tight tendons along her neck. The stress of so many weeks flowed down her spine and away from her body. "This really is heavenly and just what I needed." Her mind went a little fuzzy with relaxation, and her eyes slid closed, voice getting softer with each word. "Funny how I never thought about how little actual physical contact I have in my life these days. Not even hugs…"

Every deep breath she drew filled her with the scent of peppermint, sage and Alex's aftershave. The relaxing massage, the tempting smells and images of this oh-so-physical man made her warm with pleasure.

There was something intimate about sharing this experience together, yet safe because nothing more could happen while they were being massaged. But during the dinner cruise tonight? And afterward?

She'd already broken so many personal rules when it came to this man. How much further could he entice her to go?

Five

Alex knocked on the cabin door, a bouquet of wild-flowers in his hand, wrapped in paper and tied with some kind of string the lodge gift shop had called raffia. He'd even written a card for her, including a poem he'd found in French about a beautiful woman. He wanted to make the flowers special, more personal.

If ever a woman needed some pampering, it was Nina.

That instant during the massage when she'd commented on how rarely she was touched had been a serious gut check moment of all the things she was missing in her life, down to the simplest—touches. He'd witnessed firsthand how hard she worked for her son, how she'd restructured her whole life to be his first and fiercest advocate all on her own. Alex burned with the need to make her life easier.

At the same time, all this made him nervous after Johanna's rejection. And now with Nina, it meant even more that things go well. He wanted to get this right, all the way down to a French poem.

The door opened and he felt the wind knocked clear out of him as surely as if he'd been thrown off a bull. "You look…amazing."

His eyes swept over her, her red curls gathered up into a loose bunch on top of her head, one curl trailing down her cheek. She wore a simple black wraparound dress that brushed the top of her knees. He recognized the long gold chain from the ranch's jewelry store. His pulse ramped up at the thought of her going to extra trouble to prepare for their date.

"It's nothing fancy. I didn't pack with a dinner cruise in mind." She toyed with the link chain, stepping back.

"If this is simple, I'm not sure my heart can take anything more." Truth.

"Save the bull for the rodeo ring." She laughed, taking the flowers from him and burying her face in the bouquet. "Thank you, they're lovely. I'll put them in water while I get my shoes. Sorry I'm not ready yet, but you are early," she called over her shoulder as she walked to the kitchen.

His eyes held on the gentle sway of her hips. He ached to walk up behind her and brush a kiss along the vulnerable curve of her neck.

"I came early to introduce you to the sitter, who ought to be here in just a minute. I thought it would be best if I brought her by to spend time with Cody before he goes to sleep, in case he wakes up while you're gone." He peered out the window to check for the caregiver, then sat beside Cody at the kitchen table where the boy drew using an iPad program.

His little fingers flew across the screen tracing lines, picking and shading with different colors. His concentration was so intense his wiry body didn't move other than for his tiny fingertips. He wore cowboy PJs, and his blond hair was spiky wet from a bath.

Nina turned on the faucet and filled a hammered metal pitcher with water, the flowers already tucked inside. "That's very thoughtful—and insightful. Thank you. I had planned to speak with her, of course, but having Cody meet her is even better. Is she one of the camp counselors?"

Alex glanced out the window again and stood to get the door for their guest. "Actually I brought the best babysitter I know. The one I trust above all others." He tugged the door open and waved her inside. "This is my sister, Amie."

The impulse to ask Amie had surprised him. His sister had merely hummed knowingly, seeing right through him. But she hadn't pumped him for information about the date. She'd merely asked what time.

His twin rushed into the cabin in a swirl of perfume and some long shirt-dress thing. Funny how she always said she hated the beauty pageant days yet she still glammed up like the runway queen she'd once been.

She hugged her brother quickly before walking to Nina standing stunned at the sink. "I'm Amethyst— Amie. Nice to meet you, Nina." She approached Cody more slowly, carefully, aware and sensitive. "And this must be Cody."

Nina set the pitcher in the middle of the table and

tucked the card into her purse. "My goodness, thank you for coming. I'm sorry if your brother pressured you."

"Not at all. I love kids. Although I feel robbed not to get more time with Cody, since he'll be going to sleep soon." Amie angled her head to look at his drawing.

Nina pulled a list from the counter. "I expected to have him in bed before you arrived, but I wrote down my contact info and all his favorite soothers. He has a special weighted blanket—puffy blue—for bedtime or watching TV. It's a sensory issue."

Amie took the list and placed it on the table in plain sight. "Weighted blanket. Got it." She tucked into the chair beside Cody slowly, adjusting her whirlwind demeanor. She slipped a boho bag off her shoulder and set it gently on the table. "Cody, do you like cats? I'm the cat lady around here."

"Cats?" he asked without looking up from his art project that was taking shape into a herd of horses racing in a circle around a little boy. "How many?"

"I have four at home." She held up four fingers, then pushed down two fingers, talking as if he were looking at her. "But I brought two itty-bitty kittens with me."

Cody looked to the side, toward her but not at her. Nina smiled and Alex slid an arm around her waist, whispering in her ear, "I told you she's great with kids."

Amie carefully lifted two young kittens from her boho bag. The orange tabbies wore little sweaters made of socks and were cradled in a lined box. "They stay warm by keeping close to me. These are strays we found in the barn. Actually there were four. Johanna is bottle-feeding two and I'm bottle-feeding the other two."

She pulled out a couple of tiny bottles and raised her

perfectly plucked eyebrows expectantly as she waited for his response.

"Oh," Cody gasped, rocking forward on the bench for a closer look. "Kittens? I like kittens. Cat lady has kittens and I like kittens."

Alex chuckled. "Does Stone know he's taking bottle-fed kittens on his honeymoon this weekend?"

Amie glanced up, her long black braid swinging. "They'll be weaned by then, silly. I'll have the four until they get back."

Nina leaned in to sweep a finger down each fuzzy orange back. "Will you keep them?"

"I'm not that much of a crazy cat lady. I already have four of my own." Amie cradled one in her hand and positioned the mini bottle to its mouth. "We'll get them spayed and neutered and find them good homes."

Cody sat cross-legged on his chair, the rocking barely discernible as he ran one finger along a kitten's back just as his mother had done. "So soft."

Nina cautioned, "Be careful, Cody. Gentle."

Amie scooted closer. "Would you like to feed her? I'll hold the kitten and you hold the bottle."

"Yes, yes, yes." He held out his hand, wriggling his fingers.

"Cody," Nina said. "I'll stay to tuck you in."

"Feeding the kittens. I want to feed the kittens. Don't wanna go to bed yet." His words dwindled as he took the bottle, his eyes focused on holding the bottle to the kitten's mouth. "Then gonna draw pictures of kitties."

Nina touched the top of her son's head lightly, smiling her thanks to Amie. "That sounds wonderful, Cody. You're going to have a great time with Alex's sister."

Alex's sigh of relief mixed right in with Nina's. Her

body relaxed as tangibly as earlier when they'd gotten massages. The tension drained from him, as well. Bringing his sister here had been the right call. Nina and her son fit with his family a way that boggled his mind. Things were happening fast with Nina, and he had no desire to slow down, just keep going with the ride. He would deal with his grandmother's test later.

For tonight, he would have Nina all to himself.

Nina's toes curled in her simple gold sandals as she sipped a glass of merlot on the paddle boat dinner cruise. She had a closet full of lovely dresses from her New York City days, but they were all back at her house. Yet Alex's heated looks made her feel attractive. Alive. Even in the simple way they sat in silence now, enjoying their meal under the stars. She swirled the wine in the glass, then set it back on the table as the paddle boat made its lazy way down the Trinity River, lights twinkling from houses along the shore. The dinner cruise had tables inside and outside. But she'd opted for the moonlight and a filet mignon, the evening so different from her daily life. She loved her son, but this was such a treat after so many peanut butter sandwiches.

Things had felt so easy these past two days. Exciting and restful all at once. Alex had a slow swagger approach to life that seemed to accomplish so much more than anyone else racing around.

His twin sister had that same gift, but with a Bohemian flair instead of the down-to-earth cowboy ways of her brother. Nina had been stunned to see Amie show up in a sparkly long shirt worn as a dress along with thousands of dollars' worth of bracelets and draped necklaces. She didn't look much like a babysitter. But she'd brought orphaned kittens, teaching Cody to connect with other living beings.

There was something unique, something special about this family. And they were drawing Nina in despite the wealth and privilege, despite all the things she'd swore wouldn't be a part of her life again.

The engine roared, shifting gears as the paddle boat angled around a bend in the river. The tables were bolted to the floor, even though the glide across the water was smooth. Electric sconces flickered like candlelight in the centerpieces. Seating was limited, exclusive, only a couple of dozen tables total. Each corner offered privacy and intimacy, with the strain of live music muffling other conversation. How many proposals had been made on this riverboat?

And where had that thought come from?

She searched for something benign to say so her thoughts would stop wandering crazy paths. "Your sister is nice. You two appear to be close."

"Very close. We're twins."

The slap of the water against the hull mixed with the ragtime tunes from the musicians.

"Right, of course there's a special bond between the two of you." She tore at a roll, pinching off a bite. "Where are your parents? I haven't seen them around."

His face neutral, he answered, "They travel a lot. My father is a trust fund baby through and through. He has an office and little responsibility. My mom enjoys the finer things in life."

"I thought perhaps your father had retired, since you and your cousin run things."

Alex choked on his water. "The notion of putting my father in charge of a lemonade stand is scary." He shuddered, setting his glass back on the table. "You'll see them when they come for the wedding."

She set her roll down carefully. "Excuse me?"

"At Stone and Johanna's wedding this weekend. My parents are flying in." He smiled darkly. "They're big on showing up for the parties and flying away to the next vacation when things are tough."

She reached for his hand to offer comfort, but he leaned back and took his drink again in a not too subtle avoidance of sympathy. That simple gesture tugged at her heart even more than his words.

He drained the rest of his wine and set his glass down again. "Do you have any siblings?"

She considered pushing the point, then shook her head. "I'm an only child with no cousins." She'd hoped to have a big family of her own, with lots of siblings for Cody. "My parents had me late in life. They'd given up on ever having a child and wow, I surprised them. I know they love me, but they had such a deep routine by the time I came along, I definitely upset the apple cart—"

She stopped short as a waiter silently tucked in to refill their wineglasses before slipping away.

Alex turned the crystal goblet on the table. "You mentioned they'd retired to Arizona. I'm sorry they aren't here for you now as you parent alone. The support of family would make life easier for you."

"We're doing fine on our own." How strange that she and Alex had more in common than she'd thought. Both raised by distant parents who didn't quite know what to do with their kids. But there was so much more about him she didn't understand and so little time for this fling of hers.

"What?" he asked, the clink of silverware echoing from the next table. "Do I have food in my teeth?"

"Sorry to stare." She laughed softly, the wine and night air loosening her inhibitions enough to admit, "I'm just pensive tonight. I'm curious. Why are you going to all this trouble to romance me when I'm leaving so soon? I believe you when you say you don't use the camp for easy pickups. So what's going on here?"

"Is there something wrong with wanting to spend time with you?" Her charmer cowboy had returned; the storm clouds in his eyes from mentions of his parents long gone. "I enjoy talking to you and honest to God, it's been a while since I've found someone who piqued my interest."

"And that's all there is to it?" She leaned both elbows on the table, resting her chin in her hands while she searched for answers in his blue eyes...

And within herself, as well.

He met her gaze dead-on. "I'm attracted to you. I don't think I'm wrong in believing you feel the same. So we're dating. We have limited time together, so I'm cramming a lot of dates into one week."

"That's true." The wind stirred, carrying the strains of music and hints of lovebird conversations from a couple of tables over.

He toyed with her hand doing that tempting little move massaging her palm. "And for two of those evenings I'm already committed to attending my cousin's rehearsal dinner and wedding. I'm hoping you'll be my date for both events."

In spite of the warm summer evening, her skin chilled. "Is that what this romance is all about? Winning me over so you'll have a date for the wedding?"

"No, God. Of course not," he answered with undeniable sincerity. "I would have asked you out this week regardless."

She wanted to believe him, but then she'd believed her husband right up to the moment he rejected their child and walked out the door. "You can be honest with me. I prefer to know the truth."

"I am being honest about wanting to ask you out." He hesitated, jazz filling the silence until he continued. "And yes, it'll be nice to have you there to ease any awkwardness in my family. I briefly dated the bride."

"Ouch." Nina winced. "That could be uncomfortable to say the least."

He waved a hand. "Stone, Johanna and I have all made peace about this. I just don't want others assuming things that aren't true. Any feelings I had for her were passing and are over."

She saw only honesty in his eyes, his words ringing true. And even if he did still carry a bit of a torch for the bride, shouldn't that be a relief? It would make this week less complicated. Nina could have her romantic fling with no worries of entanglement.

So, why did she still feel a slight twinge of jealousy? Pride urged her to make light of it. "If you need me as a shield of sorts, you don't have to go to all of this trouble. Just say so and I'll be your amorous date. I'll pick up an incredibly sexy dress and look adoringly into your eyes."

"Nina, stop." He held her hand firmly and stared straight into her eyes. "I want to be here with you. And I want you to be my date for the rehearsal party and wedding because I enjoy your company."

She scrunched her nose. "Forget I said anything. Let's talk about something else."

"No, I need to be honest about this and I need for you to believe me."

"Good, because honesty is the most important thing to me."

He glanced down for an instant before meeting her eyes again. "If there wasn't wedding, I would still be asking you out, pursuing the hell out of you, because you are a fascinating woman. And please, please find that incredibly sexy dress. Except it will be me and the other men there staring at you." He lifted her hand and kissed her knuckles. "Now, would you like to dance before they serve dessert?"

"Yes, I would like that very much." She squeezed his hand and stood, letting the music tug her along with his words. Because all those jealous thoughts and wondering what he might be up to didn't matter. Tonight was a rare treat. To be out and romanced.

The band segued into a slow song as if anticipating her preference…her need. The small dance floor already held four other couples, but everyone was in their own private world. She'd thought she had that with Warren. God, she'd been so wrong.

Shaking off thoughts of her ex, she stepped into Alex's arms, determined to enjoy the night and stop thinking about the future. The heat of his palm on her back urged her closer, until her breasts skimmed his chest. He tucked her near him, resting his chin against her temple, the rasp of his late-day beard perfectly intimate against her skin.

No words were needed and in fact, she didn't want to speak. She soaked up the manly sensation that had been so lacking in her life for so long, the scent of Alex's aftershave mixing with a hint of musk. The strong play of his muscles under her hands as they danced. Her body flamed to life. Embers so long buried she'd assumed them cold and dead were stoked to life, igniting a passion. And not just for any man. She wanted Alex. This week was her only time with Alex McNair, and she should make the most of it.

The absolute most.

Something had shifted in Nina between the main course and dessert. She'd become…intense. All he'd done was ask her to his cousin's wedding. She hadn't even read the French poem yet. She'd tucked it in her purse, and as far as he could tell, she hadn't taken it back out.

He walked silently beside her up the flagstone walkway to her cabin. She hummed the music from the boat but didn't speak and wasn't sure where they were headed next. Especially after that out-of-the-blue outburst of hers offering to be his arm candy at his cousin's wedding.

Her speech would be burned in his memories as one of his favorite moments in life. Ever. She was amazing. Sexy and funny. Loyal. They hadn't known each other long, but in two days she'd turned his world upside down until he couldn't stop thinking about her.

Although there was still the issue of her son's stocks. She didn't even appear to know Cody had them or she would have said something. Her not knowing would only make it harder for him to offer to buy them.

Alex was a businessman, a damn good one. He always had a plan—everything from a five-year plan down to a plan for the day. But with Nina, he'd been flying by the seat of his pants without even reins to hold on to. He wasn't normally impulsive, but Nina made him want to forge ahead, throwing away rationales and agendas. He would figure out the issue of his grandmother's quest later. It would all come together. It had to.

The creak of the rocking chair sliced through the night sounds. His sister sat on the front porch under the outdoor light.

The former beauty pageant queen spread her hands. "Welcome home. You should have stayed out later." She carefully tucked her padded box with kittens back into her boho bag. Long fingers that had once played the piano to accompany her singing now crafted high-end jewelry. "Cody was an angel. We fed the kittens. Then he drew pictures of them. There's one for you on the counter, and I hope you don't mind that I kept one for myself. He's a regular little Picasso."

Nina grabbed the banister and walked up the steps. "Surely it wasn't that easy."

"He woke up once, asked for a glass of water. He really wanted to feed the kittens again." She adjusted her back, bracelets jingling. "I didn't think you would mind, so I let him, and then he went right back to sleep. We had fun. Truly."

Nina took Amie's hands. "I can't thank you enough for making the evening special for him too. Change is difficult for him, but you made the night magical with your kittens. I wish I'd thought to take a picture."

"Don't worry. We took tons of selfies. I'll forward them to you. I mean it when I say I enjoyed myself. I'll bring the kittens by again." She tipped her head to the side. "I would like to do a sketch of him, if that's okay with you."

"Of course."

"Good. It's a plan. I have this week off work for the wedding, so I'll see you around." Amie swept in a swirl of elegance. "Good night, you two. I'm going to head back before I turn into a pumpkin."

His sister patted him on the face as she walked down the steps, brushing aside his thanks before she wound her way back to the main house.

He turned to Nina to ask if she and Cody would go on a ride with him tomorrow, but before he could speak, she kissed him. Not just a quick kiss or peck on the cheek. She wrapped her arms around his neck and pressed flush against him. Her mouth parting, welcoming and seeking. And he damn well wasn't saying no.

Moving her closer, taking in the give of her soft curves, he deepened the kiss, sweeping his tongue against hers. Tasting and exploring. Wanting. The chemistry between them had been explosive from the first moment he'd laid eyes on her. With Nina, he was alive in the moment—the future be damned.

A throaty moan of pleasure vibrated through her into him. This kiss was the kind a couple shared when there was going to be more. But while he'd known things were moving fast between them, he hadn't expected to move this quickly. Her hands slid over his shoulders, digging into his shirt, sliding lower.

Sweeping back her hair, he kissed along her jaw. "This is not the reaction I expected."

"Good." Her head fell back to give him freer access, the gold links of her delicate necklace glinting in the porch light against her pale skin. "The last thing I ever want to be is predictable."

He trailed one finger along the path of those gold links, lower down her throat and collarbone, all the way to the curve of her breast. A slow shiver went through her, and it was all he could do not to put his mouth on the leaping pulse at the base of her throat.

"You're so incredible. You damn near bring me to my knees." Even if he hadn't come close to understanding her yet... God, how he wanted to.

She toyed with the top button of his shirt, as breathless from the touches as he was. "What if I said I don't care about your money and I don't have room in my life for another person? But I'm okay with having a fling this week?"

His body shouted hell yes, but his brain insisted this was too good to be true. And what if he wanted more than a week? How had she turned the tables on him so quickly? "You're really propositioning me? For the week only?"

"You may not believe me, but I don't do this kind of thing often." She nibbled her bottom lip. "But there's chemistry between us. With this window of time away from the rest of the world, it seems meant to be. For now."

He looked for doubt or hesitation in her green eyes and found fire instead. Pure fire. "When do you propose we start this fling?"

She wriggled closer, backing him toward the cabin door. "What about now?"

Six

She was actually doing this. Having her first official fling.

Sure, she'd been married, but she'd dated her husband for nearly a year before sleeping with him and he'd been her first. Her only. Even the thought of Warren threatened to freeze her with nerves, so she pushed away those memories. Nothing would steal this opportunity from her. This was a fantasy getaway with a fantasy-worthy man, a slice of time away from the real world. She deserved this. Needed it, even, with a physical ache she hadn't known was there until Alex made her feel all that she was missing.

Nina reached behind her to fumble for the cabin door without ending the kiss. She was an adult with few chances to feel like a woman anymore. Right now, with Alex's hands cupping her bottom, she wasn't sure she'd ever felt like this before.

He nibbled her bottom lip. "I'll get that."

Before he finished the sentence, he'd swung the door wide, his hands returning fast to her bottom. He lifted her until her feet dangled and he walked her across the threshold. One step at a time, he moved deeper into the room until the backs of her thighs hit the sofa and he lowered her, leaning with her and stretching out over her. All of it so fluid they never broke contact. Her nerves hummed with arousal from the weight of him. His hands tangled in her hair as he kissed her deeply, thoroughly.

Her body ached for release. Not just release, because she could take care of that alone, but the completion that came from sex. From a man's hands on her body. From this man's hands.

He angled up onto his elbows, murmuring against her neck. "I don't want to crush you."

Her fingers skittered down his back, tugging his shirt from his pants. "I like the feel of you on top of me."

In particular the warm press of his muscular thigh between her legs. She arched her hips ever so slightly. Pleasure rippled through her.

Alex picked up on the nuance and nudged closer. "And I like being here."

She purred her approval against his mouth. "Thank you for the flowers."

The wildflowers' sweet perfume mingled with the rustic air of the log cabin. And there was that note she'd never gotten to read. What had he written to her?

Alex stroked her hair back from her face. "You deserve more pampering."

"You've pampered me to bits today."

"I have plans for tomorrow, if you're game."

"Let's focus on the right now."

"And what is it you need, Nina?"

"More of this." She skimmed her mouth over his. "And this…" She tucked her hands into the waistband of his slacks. "And this…"

She writhed against his leg, the pressure giving the perfect stimulation to the aching bundle of nerves. His growl of appreciation sent molten desire pumping through her veins. She met him kiss for kiss, stroke for stroke, exploring the feel of his hard-muscled body. She kept waiting for him to steer them toward the bedroom, but he seemed content to make out—with some seriously heavy petting. His hand smoothed aside the top to her wraparound dress, his fingers tucking inside her bra. The rasp of his work-roughened fingertips sent sparks shimmering along her skin, her nipples pulling tight.

She couldn't remember how long it had been since she indulged in just old-fashioned necking. He was stroking her to a fever pitch, her body moving restlessly under him.

"Alex," she whispered, "let's move to the bedroom."

Or to the spa tub in her bathroom. Her imagination took flight, the naked visions in her mind bringing her closer to the edge. Still, Alex didn't move to leave the sofa. In fact, his head dipped and he captured her nipple in his mouth, rolling it with his tongue and teasing gently with his teeth. Her back arched into the sensation, pressing her more firmly against his leg.

Bunching the hem of her dress in his hand, Alex skimmed against her panties. She thought about her mismatched bra and undies, wishing she'd indulged in some new lingerie at the gift shop instead of a necklace.

Then she felt the full attention of his eyes focused on her as he dipped inside her panties. The intensity in his eyes relayed how much he wanted to make this happen for her. That care aroused her every bit as much as his skilled fingers stroking her until she couldn't hold back the orgasm exploding inside her. She bit her lip to hold back her cries of completion as he caressed every last aftershock from her. With a final shiver, she sagged back against the leather sofa, her body melting into the cushions with the bliss of completion.

Her breath came in ragged gasps and she dimly registered him smoothing her clothes back into place. Then he stood and cool air washed over her. She elbowed upward and he touched her shoulder lightly.

"Shhh, just relax." He kissed her on the forehead, pulled the unopened card out of her purse and set it beside the pitcher of flowers on the coffee table. "Good night, Nina. Lock up after me."

Before she could collect her stunned thoughts, he'd left. Shock chilled the pleasure as she lay on the sofa, her arms sprawled and one leg dangling off the side. What the hell had just happened?

She gathered her dress together and sat upright. Alex was definitely the most confusing man she'd ever encountered. Not that she was doing any good at understanding herself these days either.

She swept aside her tousled curls and reached for the card on the coffee table. She popped the seal and withdrew a folded piece of paper, not a card at all. But a poem written in French. Her eyes scanned and translated…the romantic words about an ode to a beautiful woman.

Her fingers crimpled the edges of the paper as the words soaked into her brain.

She'd just convinced herself to have her very first fling. But she'd indulged with a gentleman bent on romancing her.

Walking away from Nina took every ounce of self-discipline Alex possessed. But the night had spun out of control and he needed time and distance to plan his next move with her.

He jogged down her porch steps, putting space between him and the mind-blowing image of her sated on the sofa. Yes, he wanted her—so damn much his teeth hurt—but he hadn't expected her to offer a fling. And he certainly hadn't expected to start caring about her and her son. Ducking under a low branch, he made faster tracks through the trees on his way back to the lodge, glowing just ahead.

Pursuing a relationship with Nina was a train wreck in the making. Eventually she would find out about his pursuit of the shares in Cody's trust fund—the details of which his grandmother had emailed to him this afternoon. So much so he felt like a damn financial voyeur. His grandmother could lose the company if he told Nina now and she walked away.

It wasn't just about keeping the ranch for himself. He would do anything to make Gran's final days peaceful. Now he'd put all that at risk by starting a relationship with Nina. And he couldn't deny the truth. He didn't regret pursuing her, not for a second, and he had no intention of stopping.

He halted midstride, his eyes narrowing. Turning on his boot heels, away from the house, he walked toward the stables instead. With luck a midnight ride would burn off the steam building inside him.

Because the next time he faced Nina, he needed to be absolutely calm and in control of himself.

"Horse rides, Mama. Horse rides," Cody chanted the whole way from lunch to the afternoon activity, clutching Nina's hand so tightly her fingers went numb.

The sun baked the ground dry as she led Cody from the picnic area to the stables. Nina's nerves were shot. She hadn't slept the night before, tossing and turning, wondering why Alex had walked away from her. She hadn't heard from him or seen him all morning. She wondered if they were still on for their plans he'd mentioned the night before. He'd said he wanted to see her and she'd agreed.

She absently chewed her already short nails. Her son had been wound like a top since he woke up. For the past few days they'd ridden ponies and worked on their equine skills. Today, he would ride a larger horse.

Nina's stomach was full of butterflies. She knew he was ready, but still. She tried not to let her own fear of horses taint the experience for him.

As she neared the corral, children clustered around their counselors, each camper wearing a different color shirt according to the group. Cody broke free and raced to his teacher. His confidence was already growing. And his joy. Even an inkling of joy from her pensive son was pure shimmering gold.

Parents had been encouraged to step back today, so Nina stopped by the split-rail fence.

"Hello, Nina?" Amie's voice called to her through the masses.

Nina searched the faces down the line along the rail. She angled and walked past other parents until she reached Alex's sister, standing with another woman. Part of Nina winced at the possibility Amie might ask about the date, but another part of her insisted this was an opportunity to learn more about Alex. And hopefully figure out her own feelings in the process.

"Hello," Nina said. "Thank you again for babysitting last night."

"My pleasure, truly." Amie set her sketch pad on the corral railing and hooked arms with the other woman. "Let me introduce you to Johanna Fletcher, soon to be Johanna McNair. You wouldn't know she's supposed to be the pampered bride. She insists on working in the stables right up to the day before the wedding. Johanna, this is Nina Lowery. Her son is that adorable little blond-haired camper over there—the one I told you I want to draw a sketch of today."

Nina stifled a gasp as she realized this was the woman Alex had mentioned briefly dating. Curiosity and something greener prompted Nina to study the leggy, down-to-earth woman. Johanna and Amie were total opposites, yet there was a scrubbed-clean glamor to Johanna in her frayed jeans, worn boots and baggy T-shirt.

Johanna laughed, swishing her blond braid over her shoulder. "The substitute vet tech doesn't arrive until then. I'm here for my animals. Stone knows that."

Nina shook off the jealous thoughts and searched for something to say. "This camp you and your fiancé have started is simply amazing."

Johanna's smile beamed. "We both consider ourselves lucky to have the means and opportunity to make a difference for children."

"Well, you certainly have made a difference for Cody. I'm grateful your staff was able to fit us in at the last minute when I called on Wednesday."

Johanna's forehead creased for a moment before she smiled again, stepping back. "Well, I should get to work. Amie, we can talk about the extra guests later." She waved quickly. "Nice to meet you, Nina."

Nina waited until the vet tech was out of sight before turning to Amie. "Did I say something wrong?"

"Not at all. I think she was just confused over how you got into the camp last week. There's usually a long waiting list."

"Oh, good, I was afraid I'd made things awkward, since she dated Alex."

Amie arched a perfectly plucked eyebrow. "You know about that? Not many do."

"He mentioned it to me."

"How interesting that he told you." Amie leaned back against the rail, her turquoise and pewter necklace glinting in the afternoon sun. "She and Alex went out once, purely platonic, though, because she was still on the rebound from a breakup with Stone. She also didn't want to cause trouble between the cousins. And truth be told, she never really got over the crush she had on Stone. Clearly."

"Crush?"

"She practically grew up here. Her father was the stable vet tech before her. Johanna has loved Stone for as long as I can remember. Sometimes romance happens slowly over years." Amie toyed with her turquoise necklace, her eyes pensive. "And sometimes that connection happens in an instant."

"My parents were the love-since-childhood sort." She remembered her plan to find out more about Alex and asked, "What about yours?"

Amie's smile went tight. "They met in college. My mother always said the second she met him, she knew he would be hers. My father was considered a catch and my mom is quite competitive."

How did a person respond diplomatically to that? "From the tone of your voice, I take it to mean competitive isn't a good thing."

"Not in her case." She snorted inelegantly. "She may truly love Dad, but she sure loves his money. It's weird to think how she likes the wealth but carries this huge chip on her shoulder, insecure from feeling that she never accomplished anything on her own. So she pushed us to find the success she felt she'd been cheated out of by living the life as a cossetted queen with a sugar daddy."

Whoa. Nina rocked back on her boot heels. "That's... unfortunate."

"Don't feel sorry for her. You haven't met my mom." Amie crossed her feet at the ankles, her brown riding boots immaculate. "Have you ever watched that reality show series about babies in beauty pageants? That was my life. From the beaded gowns to the questionably adult dance routines to pixie stix poured into cola to keep me awake at nap time."

"For real?"

"I have shelves of tiaras and trophies to prove it." She straightened and struck a quick beauty queen pose. "I even have a special row for my fake teeth she had made when my baby teeth fell out."

There was something sad about not enjoying the precious gap-toothed smile of an innocent child. "It doesn't sound like you were on board with those plans."

"I'm only marginally messed up by her stage mom ways." Amie waved aside Nina's concern. "I went to college and double-majored in art and business. I wasn't summa cum laude, but I finished on time. I have a job. Alex is the one who had it far tougher than I did."

Nina's stomach clenched. "What do you mean?"

Amie glanced into the corral where children were being lifted onto placid mares and ponies. "Have you ever watched the rodeo circuit? It was sure nothing like that. Before the age of eighteen, my brother had broken more bones than an adult football player. Or at least it seemed that way. And to keep our parents happy, he kept climbing right back on again."

Nina pressed a hand to her tight throat, thinking about her son's joy today and envisioning Alex as a child being pushed by adults. "I'm so sorry. For both of you."

"Don't be." Amie shrugged an elegant shoulder dismissively. "We didn't starve. We weren't abused. We lived a life of privilege and accolades. I just wanted you to understand why sometimes we're a little bit off when it comes to relationships and expressing our feelings."

Nina wasn't sure what to say in response, looking around nervously, seeing a pigtailed girl with muscular dystrophy benefitting from the rhythm of the dun-colored pony she rode. The girl smiled from the saddle, her eyes dancing with each step of the pudgy pony. An older boy missing an arm worked on his balance riding a surefooted mare. Kicking up a steady stream of clay, the blue roan mare walked around the pen, seemingly sensitive to the needs of the boy.

Alex and his sister downplayed themselves and their lives, but this family clearly worked to use their money and power for good. And this clearly good woman was sharing so much about herself and their family. Nina felt like a fraud.

"Alex and I have only known each other for a few days," Nina blurted out.

"Right." Amie picked up her sketch pad off the rail and backed away one poised step at a time. "Like I said, some fall faster than others." With a wave, she spun away, sketch pad under her arm.

Nerves clustered in Nina's stomach over the mention of relationships and commitments. No surprise, since her ex had trounced her ability to trust. This was supposed to be a fling.

And yet she couldn't help searching the grounds for a glimpse of him.

A rush of warm air over her neck gave her only an instant's warning before...

"Good afternoon, beautiful."

Alex braced his hands on Nina's waist as she turned fast to face him. Waiting to touch her again had made for a torturous twelve hours. He'd always considered himself a methodical man, but in a few short days this woman had flipped his world upside down.

His late-night ride hadn't helped him find any answers for balancing his grandmother's request and his driving desire to pursue Nina for more than just one night. Until he came up with the right approach for addressing the stock purchase, he wanted to do everything in his power to win her over, not just physically.

Her eyes were wary as she met his. "Thank you. I wondered where you were this morning."

"Taking care of business for the wedding." He stroked her waist lightly. "Now I have a couple of hours this afternoon free to spend with you."

Her chin went up. "If you think we're just going to pick up where we left off after you walked out without—"

He tapped her lips. "I have other plans for the day and hope you're amenable."

"To what?" she asked warily.

"A tour of the McNair property while your son's busy with his lessons." Maybe then she would understand how important the ranch was to him, and then she would understand how this legacy compelled him. "Amie is staying nearby in case Cody needs anything. She said it's the perfect opportunity to sketch him."

"You've thought of everything." She looked around. "Are we going on a drive?"

He shook his head slowly. "Your son is riding today. I think he would be proud to see his mom give it a go, as well."

Her nose crinkled. "You're playing dirty pool, using guilt on me.

"Is it working? Because your chariot awaits, beautiful lady." He stepped aside, gesturing behind him.

Her eyes went to the large bay-and-white horse behind him. The gelding was tied to a rail post swishing his tail from side to side. Nina studied the horse incredulously.

"Do you actually expect me to ride him?" Her voice

squeaked, her wide eyes still fixed on the bay. Not surprisingly, the gelding's tack was gorgeous. The light tan saddle contained an elegant inlaid depiction of a horse herd at a full-out gallop. The cantle, skirt and fender were plated with etched silver, complementing the plates of silver ornamentation on the bridle. Alex and the bay looked like a scene from an old Western movie. Yippee-ki-yay indeed.

"I thought we could both ride together and that would make you feel more secure in the saddle." Had he pushed too hard? It had seemed like a good idea this morning.

She glanced over at her son, then back at the horse. The gelding was calm enough that Nina didn't run screaming in the other direction.

Chewing her lip, she nodded tightly. "Okay, sure. If Cody can conquer his fears to step out in public, I can do this."

Alex slid his hand behind her neck. "Nina, you are so damn incredible."

"Yeah, yeah, whatever." She grabbed his arms and tugged him toward the horse. "Now hurry up before I change my mind."

With a cowboy whoop, he grasped her waist and lifted her over the split-rail fence. He took his time setting her on her feet again, letting her slide down the length of his body. The press of her soft curves and the swing of her red wavy curls had his body on fire in an instant. He didn't regret walking away last night, but he sure as hell looked forward to the day he wouldn't have to.

"Nina, this is Zircon. He's an American paint." He stroked the white horse with brown markings. Zircon's

nearly solid brown face was interrupted by a long cres-
cent stripe below his right eye. Zircon shook his head,
a rumble that radiated all the way to his tail. He looked
lazily at Alex, tongue hanging out of the right side of
his mouth. "He's solid and sweet as you can tell. I trust
him with a second rider, but we'll keep it short for him
and for you. Are you ready?" Alex touched Zircon's
tongue and the horse came to full attention, tongue
back in the cheek.

Alex waited for her verdict. She glanced at her son,
clearly in his element, atop a horse. And sure enough,
Amie sat with her back against a tree, sketch pad in
hand.

Alex gripped Nina's elbow. "He's fine. Happy. He'll
be busy for the next hour on a scripted walk to the creek
and back. What about you?"

"Yes, let's do this before I lose my nerve." She
pressed her hand to the horse's body and slid her foot
into Alex's linked fingers.

She was tense and not particularly pliable, but he'd
helped worse. He hefted her up and secured her, quickly
mounting up behind her.

Zircon stood steady. Not a move. "Good boy," he
praised softly before sliding his arms around Nina, his
cheek against her hair. "How are you doing?"

"You have experience if this horse freaks out.
Right?"

"Of course." He breathed in the berry smell of her
shampoo as he clicked for the horse to start forward.

"Okay, good." She grabbed the pommel and horn
fast. "You know there are a half dozen women around
here who are green with envy—and not afraid of
horses."

"Where? I don't see anyone but you." He slid a palm to her stomach and urged her to lean into the circle of his arms. "You still aren't relaxing. Why don't you grab a chunk of mane with one of your hands? It'll help you connect to Zircon and you'll gain some more balance."

"Truthfully?" she said through her teeth. "I'm trying to figure out why you're doing this, since you left last night when I made it clear you could stay."

Her right hand moved toward Zircon's mane. She twined her fingers around the locks of bay-and-white mane, her breathing easing ever so slightly.

"You did." He rested his chin on her head, looking out at the grassy stretch of earth, the creek, the trees that had lived here longer than he had. Zircon walked on calmly, responding to the slight pressure in Alex's legs. He started to angle the horse toward the open field. Toward where he and Nina could talk. He was torn between this woman and his obligation to this land. "And there will come a day when I take you up on that."

"But not last night." Her back went starchy stiff against his chest.

"There's a difference between thinking you're ready to take a step and actually being ready." Arm wrapped around her, he urged her closer.

The press of her bottom against him was sweet torture. The roll of the horse's steps moved Nina's body against him until he throbbed with arousal. A low growl slipped between his clenched teeth.

She laughed softly. "Serves you right."

"Well, damn. I think I irked your feelings. Sorry about that." He chuckled softly. His arm slid up just under her breasts. "I guess we'll have to…talk and get to know each other better."

She tipped her head, her expression quizzical. "Talking would be good. Tell me more about what it was like growing up here."

"Well, my grandmother believed we needed to learn every inch of the farm firsthand." He guided the horse around a fallen tree and into an open field of bluebonnets. Zircon's ears flicked back and forth. "We shadowed the staff. Sometimes it was fun, sometimes not so much. She said she didn't want any spoiled trust fund babies taking over the family business."

"Good for her."

He nudged Zircon to the left past a fat oak, birds flapping from the trees up into the clear Texas sky. "One summer she got us all chickens and we learned to start a chicken coop."

"Seriously?" She relaxed against him, laughing.

"To this day we call that 'the Summer of Eggs.' We had to collect them and learned how to cook the eggs as well—scrambled, fried, then graduating to omelets and quiche."

"I like that your grandmother had you boys learn, as well."

Did she know that she'd loosened her grip on the horn, and one hand had slid to rest on her thigh? He didn't intend to point that out. Her shoulders and body started to move with Zircon's gait and not against it. Nina was a natural when fear wasn't her main focus.

"She and my grandfather built this business from the ground up." As the words rolled from his tongue, he realized his reason for bringing her here. It wasn't about riding a horse. It was about hoping she would understand his motives. Hoping that she would be able to forgive him for holding back part of his reason for seeking her out. "The ranch is actually Gran's. My grandfather was the jeweler/craftsman. Together they blended that dream into an empire." Alex's neck kinked with nerves as he considered how far to take this conversation.

"That's lovely, seeing their differences as strengths to be blended."

"You said your husband grew up pampered."

"Did I?"

"I believe so. You mentioned his wealthy parents and their need to control." He swallowed hard before venturing into that damn dangerous territory. "Would that be the Lowerys of Lowery Resorts?"

She glanced back in surprise. "Yes, actually they are. Cody too, since he inherited his father's portion of the holdings."

Alex forced his hands to stay loose on the reins. "And you're the executor or are his grandparents?"

"I am, and God," she sighed, sagging back into a slump, "the weight of that worries on me. The doctors still don't know exactly what the autism means for his future. Will he be able to support himself? Live on his own? I don't know the answers, so I have to be very careful with that money. He could have to live off the investments for the rest of his life."

Her words hammered at Alex with a reality he hadn't considered until now. He'd been so busy thinking about what was best for his grandmother and the ranch, he hadn't given a thought to worrying about that four-year-old boy. This wasn't about the McNairs versus the Lowerys. This involved a sick old woman and a special-needs child who might never be able to support himself. That truth sliced clean through him.

They were well beyond the bluebonnet field and

walking through a rocky, unstable area. Zircon's ears were pinned back. Guilt weighted Alex's shoulders down and dimmed the beauty of the day. So much so that he lost track of the path in the land he knew as well as his own hand.

So much so that he didn't see the arc of the rattlesnake between the horse's hooves until it was too late.

Seven

Nina's heart leaped to her throat.

She felt the horse coil beneath her, almost mimicking the motion of the rattlesnake. Zircon's muscles exploded forward and he reared back. Ears pinned flat against his head, the paint pawed the air. Alex banded one arm around her to hold her secure and the other held the reins. He said something, some kind of command to Zircon, but she could only hear the roaring in her ears and the hammering of her heart as the world tilted backward.

She was going to die. Fall off the horse. Break her neck. Make her son an orphan. She'd stepped outside her comfort zone and would pay the price. A scream welled in her throat. She squeezed her eyes closed to fight vertigo, every muscle in her body tensing. She grabbed a fistful of mane, holding so tightly that her knuckles were bone white.

Zircon's hooves slammed down again, jarring her teeth, pushing her forward and off balance. She tried to stabilize her body weight on Zircon's neck but barely caught her breath before the horse bolted forward. She slammed back against the hard wall of Alex's chest, knocking the air from her lungs.

"Alex!" she choked out.

"Stay calm," his voice rumbled against her ear. "Hold tight and remember to breathe."

Faster and faster, the horse galloped along the path, then off. Zircon's gait was hurried, erratic. The horse was hardly running in a straight line and his ears were still pinned in fright. Earth and dirt flew past her vision. They raced through an open field, toward a creek. The wind whipped through her hair, but she hadn't been tossed off. She wasn't dead from a broken neck.

Yet.

Alex had her locked firmly against his chest, and her heartbeat raced as fast as the horse. "It's okay, Nina. I've got this. You're all right. Zircon will run himself out. We just need to stay seated."

She heard him and slowly began to believe him. Her nerves battled with a long-buried urge to enjoy the ride and ignore the risks. Just live on the edge. Which was exactly what they were about to do as Zircon readied to cross the creek. The horse pushed off the thin creek's bank. Instinctively Nina shifted her hands up the horse's neck, grabbing its mane and leaning forward into the jump.

Zircon went flying over the creek and landed smoothly on the other side. Had she squealed or screamed again? She didn't know, but the world was sparkling. This felt like flying.

The drumming of the hooves reverberated through her as Zircon nimbly galloped around fat oak trees. They approached another clearing. Alex gathered the reins and pulled the horse's head to the right. Zircon's head turned sharply and his legs followed. Nina watched the horse's nervous eyes soften. Alex kept the horse turning to the right. The circle became smaller and smaller. Bit by bit, the horse slowed. Then stopped, snorting and pawing at the ground.

Alex slid from the saddle and lifted her off, setting her quickly on the grass before kneeling beside his horse. His hands skimmed along the front legs, left and right.

Nina covered her mouth. How could she have forgotten about the snake so quickly? "Is he okay? Was Zircon bitten?"

Alex shook his head. "It doesn't appear so, thank God. The rattler just spooked him." He glanced over his shoulder. "Are you all right?"

"I'm fine, only a little surprised. And very grateful no one was injured, especially Zircon." She reached out tentatively and patted the horse's neck, the satiny coat soothing to the touch. Frothy sweat pooled beyond the horse's ears and around the bit.

Rising, Alex stood beside her again, stroking her cheek. "I'm so damn sorry that he went out of control so fast."

"You kept us all safe. And truth be told, once I got past the initial startle, I actually enjoyed the ride. I didn't expect to feel like that."

"Like what?" He stepped closer, his hand drawing her nearer.

"My skin tingled all over," she said with only a sliver of space between them.

He smiled, the corners of his eyes crinkling. "You're a horsewoman after all."

Laughing softly, she angled closer, her nerves igniting at the simple brush of her breasts again his chest. "A horsewoman? That's taking things a little far based on one ride."

He tapped his temple. "Trust me. I have a sense for things like this."

"Perhaps next time we ride we can take things a little slower and see how it goes."

"You're willing to ride again?" he asked with clear undertones.

"Absolutely I am." Her body damn near ignited with thoughts of last night, of taking things further. "In fact, I'm looking forward to it."

"You're going to be sore after today's experience." His hands slid down her back, lower, pressing her hips to his.

"Probably. Where's your masseuse?"

"I was thinking of something else to relieve tension later tonight, if you're game."

While she wanted to be with him, she was confused after his departure the evening before. Things were moving so fast, and she was the one who'd wanted that, wanted a fling, but she needed to understand *his* intent better. She needed to make sure they were on the same page. "About last night—"

"Things moved fast, I get that."

"They did, and I have to confess I'm not used to that. So maybe I sent some mixed signals. I was married, but my life has been focused solely on my son since then.

This week has been…different. I guess what I'm trying to say is that I didn't want you to leave," she admitted. Since she was living on the edge today, she might as well go for broke.

"I didn't want to go."

Finally she asked the question that had plagued her through a very sleepless night. "Then why did you?"

He tugged his hat off—how had that stayed on through the crazy ride?—and thrust a hand through his hair. "It's difficult to explain, other than to say this week doesn't seem like long enough."

"But it's all we have." She hadn't considered more. Even the thought of being vulnerable in yet another relationship made her feel as if the world had tilted again. She backed away from him. "I have a life and a home in San Antonio."

Although that life felt mighty far away at the moment.

He slammed his hat back on his head. "You're right. Forget I said anything. Let's live in the moment."

The tension in her chest eased and she leaned against him. "One day at a time. I like that."

She arched up on her toes to kiss him, enjoying the way their mouths met with familiarity, fitting just so. His arms slid around her, his hands warm and strong palming low on her waist. Her breasts pressed to the hard wall of his chest, and her mind filled with memories of the night before, of his touch, his intuition about just how to set her on fire.

Her senses, still so alive from their mad dash, burned all the hotter. "Alex…"

"Nina…" he whispered in her ear, his beard stubble rasping against her cheek. "I want you here, now, but we're too close to the camp and there are other riders out."

She gasped, jerking away. "Oh my God, the kids are out riding." She pressed a hand to her forehead. "How could I have forgotten?"

"But we have a date for later." He pulled her back into his arms and traced her bottom lip. "I told you, I have a plan for reducing tension. Trust me?"

God, how she wanted to. "I'll see you tonight after Cody goes to sleep."

Eight hours later, Alex held his hands over Nina's eyes, hoping she would enjoy his idea for their evening together. He'd brought dinner to her and Cody first, enjoying the chance to get to know her son better. They'd eaten barbecue and played with toy horses Alex had brought as a gift until Amie arrived to babysit again.

Nina had smiled more broadly over his present to her son than she had over the chocolate strawberries he'd brought for their dessert. He couldn't help being drawn to her devotion to the boy after the way his own parents had ignored their children except for when he and Amie were trotted out to perform.

He wasn't going to have many more opportunities to be alone with Nina with his cousin's wedding right around the corner. Even the small family service would still take up all their time over the weekend, relatives pouring in left and right. Not to mention the bachelor party and rehearsal dinner.

Thoughts of family were the last kind Alex wanted right now.

Nina had made it clear she only wanted a week together, and that was likely all they would have once she knew how badly his grandmother wanted her son's shares in the McNair Corporation. He'd considered just offering an exorbitant amount of money for them, but their own finances were tangled up in investments. Selling them off to liquidate cash would be unwise fiscally, and unfair to their own investors. He was caught in a loop of damned if he did and damned if he didn't.

So he did the only thing he knew to do. Focus on letting Cody have the best camp experience possible. Get to know the child better.

And pamper Nina for whatever time they had together.

She clasped his wrists. "Where are we going?"

"Almost there," he said, stopping in front of the sauna attached to the family's private pool house. "Are you ready for more relaxation?"

"I think so."

He lowered his hands and opened the door to the small cedar room. A tray waited with water bottles beside a stack of fat towels.

Everything had been prepared as he'd ordered. "This is our family's private sauna. No one will bother us here. I thought you might be sore after being jostled around on Zircon. Your choice, though, if you'd rather not."

She turned in his arms to face him, smiling. So easy to please and so at home in the places he loved best. She fit in here seamlessly. "I think it's a fabulous idea." The emerald green of her gauzy blouse made her eyes sparkle. "You have a knack for knowing just what I need. But I'm curious, what do *you* need?"

Her provocative question hung in the air between them.

His eyes fell to the deep V of her shirt, which had

been drawing his gaze all night long. A long lock of hair had slipped loose, the curl pooling just above her breast as if it were providing a path for his touch. "I need you, Nina. Just you."

He walked her into the sauna, the temperature still moderate. For now. His temperature? Definitely notching higher the longer he looked at her.

She stroked along his shoulders, her touch making his skin tighten everywhere. "I've got to know, though, are you going to walk out on me again?"

"Not unless you ask me to." He kicked the door closed, sealing them inside the low-lit cubicle.

For good measure, he went back and locked it.

"Doubtful." She arched up on her toes to nip his bottom lip. "I'm warming it up fast." She winked at him. "I think we're both way too overdressed for this sauna idea of yours."

"I'd like to help you with that." An understatement.

She lifted her arms in an unspoken invitation for him to peel off her loose blouse. He swept up the gauzy fabric and tossed it aside on the bench, his eyes never leaving all the creamy pale skin he was unveiling.

His breath caught in his throat at the sight of her breasts in white lace. High, luscious curves. "You look every bit as beautiful as you felt last night."

He'd been reliving those moments in his head all day long. Even more, he'd been looking forward to making even more memories with her tonight.

Her fingers walked down his shirt. "You don't have to shower me with compliments."

"I want to…if I spoke as many languages as you do—" he tugged the zipper on her jeans, down, down, revealing white bikini panties "—then I could tell you again and again how beautiful you are, how much I want you, how often thoughts of you distract me at work."

"You have quite a way with words no matter what language you're speaking."

She worked free the buttons on his plaid shirt, one at a time, her knuckles grazing his skin and tempting him to toss aside restraint. Then her cool hand slid inside his jeans and restraint was absolutely the last thing on his mind. She curved her hand around his throbbing erection and he bit back a groan as she stroked.

Growling low in his throat, he eased her down to sit on the bench and knelt in front of her, tugging her boots off one, then the other. Her new leather boots were starting to have a worn-in look, as though she belonged here. In his house. In his arms.

She flowed forward, sweeping aside his loose shirt, then leaned back again, eyes roving his chest with obvious appreciation. Kicking aside his own boots, he tugged his wallet from his pocket and pulled out two condoms, then placed them on the bench.

Her pupils widened with desire.

He peeled off his socks and shucked his well-worn jeans before standing naked in front of her. Her smoky smile steamed over him hotter than the sauna. She trailed her fingers down his chest, down his stomach, gently brushing his erection. He throbbed in response, her touch sweet torture. She trailed her hand lower down his thigh, muscles contracting at her caress. Urgency pumped through his veins.

Lifting her hand, he pressed a kiss to the inside of her wrist, feeling the pulse beat hard against his lips. Then he stepped back to turn up the heat on the sauna, coils heating the stones, a water fountain trickling down to send bursts of steam. Bottles of oils lined a rack before the fountain—eucalyptus, citrus, birch and peppermint.

Choosing eucalyptus, he drizzled oil over the stones before turning back to her. Anticipation curled through him. Finally he had her all to himself, naked, alone, his for the taking. They'd been building to this moment since the first time he saw her. And in spite of all the reasons they didn't stand a chance in hell at having more, he couldn't stop wanting her.

He reached to the stack of fluffy white towels in the corner and spread two out on the bench. He reclined her back, using an extra towel to make a pillow. He stretched out over her. Flesh to flesh. His eyes slid closed for a moment.

Then thoughts gave way to sensations. The scent of her berry shampoo. The creamy softness of her neck when he pressed his lips to her pulse. She hooked her leg around his, her foot sliding up and down the back of his calf. He finally gave in to the temptation to taste her, along her shoulder, nudging aside a bra strap, then the other, baring her breasts to his mouth, his touch. She arched up with a husky moan and he reached underneath her to unhook her bra and toss it aside.

Sweat beaded along her skin, glistening. Perspiration streaked down her neck, then between her breasts. One droplet held on the tip of her nipple. He dipped his head and flicked his tongue, catching the droplet and circling, laving. Her head fell back and a moan floated from her lips.

Nina nibbled his earlobe. "No more waiting." She passed him a condom. "We can go slow after. And from the count of what you pulled from your pocket, you're intending there to be an after."

"At least that much," he vowed. "And whatever else you want."

"Perfect," she purred, trailing her fingers down his arms and guiding his hands to hurry up.

He tore open the wrapper, and her hands covered his as she helped him sheathe himself. She hitched her leg higher, hooked on his hip, bringing her moist heat closer. His forehead fell to rest against hers as he pushed inside her. Her breath came faster and faster, flowing over him. He thrust deeper, deeper still and her hips rolled against his, inviting him to continue. He thrust and she moved with him, synching into a perfect, driving rhythm that had him clenching his teeth to hold back. She'd said they could go slow next time—and there would be a next time—but he wasn't finishing now until he'd satisfied her.

The steam billowed off the rocks, filling the small room, air heavy with the scent of eucalyptus and sex. Perspiration gathered on his forehead, a droplet sliding off to hit the towel under her. Their slick bodies moved against each other, his pulse hammering in his ears. He swept her hair from her face, capturing her mouth and soaking in the feel of Nina.

Just Nina.

He braced himself on one elbow to keep his weight off her and slide his other hand between them, caressing her breasts and lower. He stroked the slick bud, circling and teasing, her purrs of pleasure urging him to continue. Just when he thought he couldn't hold out any longer, her gasps came faster and faster. Her fingernails dug into his back, scratching a light but insistent path as her head flung back. She cried out in pleasure, her orgasm pulsing around him, clasping him tighter and hurtling him over the edge into his own release.

His arm gave way and he lay fully on top of her, thrusting through the final wave of ecstasy. His breaths shuddering through him, he buried his face in her neck and rolled to his side, holding her close. Already hungry for the next time and wondering how long he could keep her here and the world at bay.

Because more than ever, he was certain that a week with Nina would never be enough.

Tucked to Alex's side, Nina trailed her fingers along his muscular arm, the scent of eucalyptus steaming through the sauna. She was already nearly halfway done with the weeklong camp. Then she would have to walk away from the Hidden Gem—from Alex.

This place was like a fairy-tale getaway, a Brigadoon, too good to be true and destined to disappear when she left. Alex made her want things she'd decided were not meant to be. Scariest of all, he made her want to risk her heart again and she didn't know if she could take another betrayal.

A sobering thought at a time she was determined to live in the moment.

She slid her hand down to link fingers with Alex. "We should get dressed soon and head back. Your sister must be getting sick of babysitting Cody."

"No hurry." He kissed their clasped hands. "Amie adores Cody and she owes me."

"For what?" she asked, hungry to know more about him.

A smile tugged at his mouth. "When we were seventeen, she didn't want to win the Miss Honey Bee

Pageant—and given how many pageants she'd won in the past, it wasn't arrogant of her to assume she would run away with that crown. But back to that time. She didn't want to go because the Honey Bee Queen had to attend the county fair and she wouldn't be able to attend homecoming."

Nina drew circles on his chest, perspiration clinging to their skin. "What did you do?"

"Nothing awful. We went boating the day before the competition, and we stayed out so long we got sunburned. I told Mom the engine stalled. Amie looked like a lobster. Mom made her compete anyway. Just slathered her in more makeup. Amie got second runner-up."

"Seriously?" The story was funny and sad all at once.

"Scout's honor." He held up his fingers. "I offered to cut her hair, but she nixed that, so we opted for the sunburn instead. I was never sure if she opted out of the haircut idea out of vanity or because Mom would have just bought a wig."

"People call you quiet and reserved, but you're really quite funny."

"I guess I have my moments." He kissed the tip of her nose, then picked up a hand towel and gently—methodically—wiped the sweat from her body. "So I take it you approve of the sauna?"

"Very much. Is there anything Hidden Gem doesn't have? Seriously, sauna, massage therapist, airplane, catered dinners, even that well-stocked gift shop, so there's no need to leave for anything. This is like nirvana."

His smile faded. "There are others who would say this place should be modernized."

"In what way? There's every convenience possible."

She couldn't imagine anywhere more restful or entertaining.

"There are no theme parks or casinos. A high-rise could fit a lot more people into the space, make more money, attract big acts to perform."

The mention of high-rise tourism made her think of her in-laws, the last people she wanted intruding on this moment. "You can't possibly agree with that. It would take away the authenticity and the charm."

"It's good to hear you say that."

The fierce intensity of his kiss took her breath away and made her wonder about the reason for his sudden shift in mood.

She gripped his shoulders, questions filling her mind. But before she could ask, a cell phone rang, jarring her. Not her ring tone. His. Sounding from his jeans on the floor.

He murmured against her mouth, "Ignore it."

Oh, how she wanted to. "It could be your sister. Cody might need me."

"You're right. Of course, we can't ignore it. I should have thought of that too."

Rolling from her, he sat on the edge of the bench and scooped his jeans from the floor. Nina stroked his broad back and traced the light scratches she'd left along his shoulder blades.

He answered the cell phone. "Amie, is something wrong with Cody?"

Alex clicked on the speakerphone and Nina sat up beside him, concern and maternal guilt chilling her warmed flesh.

"No." His sister's voice was tight with nerves. "Not at all. He's fast asleep."

Nina relaxed against him, resting her cheek on his shoulder, her hand on his chest.

"Glad to hear it," Alex said, sliding an arm around Nina. "Then what's up?"

"Prepare yourself," she said with a heavy sigh. "Mom and Dad are returning home from their trip a day early. They've already landed in Fort Worth but didn't want to make the drive out to the ranch tonight. They'll be here first thing in the morning."

His jaw tight, he turned off the speakerphone and brought the receiver to his ear. "We'll need to band together to keep things calm for Gran…"

Curiosity nipped. He'd mentioned issues with his parents, but his reaction seemed…strong. It was only a day early. Surely that wasn't a big deal. But the muscles bunching along Alex's back told her otherwise.

Nina pulled a towel from the stack and wrapped it around herself. But there was no escaping the sensation that her Brigadoon was fading.

Eight

Alex hadn't eaten breakfast yet and he already had indigestion.

He paced restlessly around the family lanai, brunch prepared, he and his sister waiting with Gran for their parents' arrival. The morning sun steamed droplets of water off the lawn from the sprinkler system. Making love with Nina had been everything he expected and more. He'd always been such a methodical man. But the instantaneous combustion between him and Nina rocked him back on his boot heels. And before he could get his bearings, his parents opted to put in an early appearance.

His mother had a way of being less than pleasant to the women he dated, which was strange, since Bayleigh McNair wasn't what anyone would call an overly adoring parent. Regardless, he didn't want Nina subjected to that, especially not now while they were still finding their way around whatever it was they had going.

A persistent crick pinched at his neck. He should have been better prepared for his parents' arrival and how he would handle them meeting Nina. They'd been due in tomorrow anyway, but he'd been taking things one day at a time this week. That sort of impulsive living wasn't his style.

Gran reclined in a patio lounger sipping tea, her breakfast untouched on the small table beside her. His indomitable grandmother was so frail she looked as if a puff of wind would whisk her away. He needed to make sure this breakfast—the whole wedding weekend—went smoothly. No drama. This was his family and they were at their best for his grandmother.

Stone's mother would be a wild card. Her behavior was always hit or miss depending on if she was using drugs or fresh out of rehab. Thus far she'd been clean for six months. If she followed past patterns, the fall was due any day now.

Maybe it wasn't fair of him to expect Nina to put up with his family's volatile dynamics, especially since weddings always multiplied drama. Except after last night with Nina, he couldn't bring himself to waste even a minute of the remaining week. He needed to persuade her they had something special—because he was going to have to come clean with her about the stocks soon.

Why couldn't Nina have come to one of the other camp sessions? Although she wouldn't be here at all if his grandmother hadn't orchestrated Nina's arrival. He couldn't imagine never having met her. So whatever it took, he would get through these next few days and maintain the peace for his grandmother.

And figure out a way to keep seeing Nina after the camp ended.

First, he had to get through welcoming his parents. They kept a suite here as well but were rarely in attendance. They preferred penthouse hotels around the world.

A limousine cruised up the oak-shaded entry road, turning toward the private drive and stopping near the lanai. While the others drank mimosas, Amie drained her simple orange juice and refilled the crystal flute. Stone and Johanna—lucky ducks—had bowed out of breakfast claiming a meeting with the caterer.

Clouds drifted over the sun as the chauffeur opened the door and Alex's mother stepped out in a flourish. Bayleigh McNair believed in making an entrance.

His mother breezed up the stairs. Collagen-puffy lips and cheek implants had changed her appearance until she looked like a distant relative of herself. Not his mother yet eerily familiar.

Alex stepped beside Gran's chair, wishing his presence alone could keep her safe and make her well. Her hand trembling, Gran set aside her teacup with a slight rattle of china, watching her grandchildren protectively. Alex patted her shoulder.

His father stepped alongside his wife, wearing a crisp suit as if he'd dressed for work. Ironic as hell, since Garnet McNair carried an in-name-only title with the company, some kind of director of overseas relations. Which just meant he could pretend he worked as he traveled the world. Mariah only requested he wine and dine possible contacts and charm them. On the company credit card of course. His parents were masters at wringing money out of Gran.

She was a savvy businesswoman, so Alex was certain she knew her son's game. And equally certain it had to break her heart, given how hard she and her husband had worked to build the family business. It was no wonder she felt the need to put her grandchildren through tests before handing over her empire.

Bayleigh swept up the lanai stairs—perfect. There was no other word to describe his mother. Not a hair out of place. Makeup fresh, a bit thicker each year. And always, always, she stayed almost skeletally thin—thanks to hours on the treadmill and a diet of cottage cheese and coffee. What the treadmill couldn't fix, she took care of with liposuction and tummy tucks. The rest of her was beige—blond hair, tanned skin, and off-white or brown clothes depending on the time of year.

He often wondered how his mom managed to keep those white outfits clean with kids around. Gran was always dusty and never minded if they'd just eaten chocolate ice cream when they gave her a hug.

Gran and Nina had a lot in common.

Bayleigh's heels clicked across the tile as she briefly hugged each of her children, leaving a fog of perfume in her wake. She dabbed her eyes with a tissue as she swooped down on her mother-in-law. "Mother McNair, how are you feeling?" She kissed Gran's cheek and then sat in a chair next to her. "I'm just so glad you're still with us for the wedding."

"No need to start digging my grave yet." Gran didn't show any irritation, only a sardonic smile of resolution. "I've got some life left in me yet."

Garnet knelt beside his mom. "Mother, please, let's not talk about unpleasantries." He took her hand in his. "I'm glad to see you looking so well, enjoying the sunshine." She glanced up at the sky. "Well, what little bit is peeking around the clouds."

Her smile turned nostalgic. "You look so much like your father, Garnet. I miss him every day even after all these years."

Although her son hadn't inherited much in the way of work ethic from his mother or father, Alex had heard his grandmother blame herself for pampering her children. He didn't agree. Not completely. She might have been indulgent in those days, but his father and aunt should have taken responsibility for their own lives. Alex passed his mother a cup of black coffee.

Bayleigh cradled the cup and inhaled the scent as if filling up on the smell alone. "We came early to help, since the bride doesn't have a mother of her own. And Mother Mariah is so very ill. Of course we all know Stone's mother can't be trusted to show up sober. So I thought I should come a day early to make sure all is in order."

Bayleigh sipped her coffee.

Garnet stayed silent, not surprising, and filled a plate with quiche and fruit. The sound of crunching footsteps sounded just before Stone jogged into sight from around the corner of the house.

Stone took the steps two at a time up to the lanai. "Sorry I'm late. Johanna is still working out details with the caterer. She'll be here when she's through. Thank you for coming, Aunt Bayleigh, Uncle Garnet." He swept his hat off and kissed his grandmother's cheek before loading up a plate of quiche, two danishes and melon slices. "I'm starving. Glad y'all saved me some food."

Amie sipped her crystal flute of orange juice. "Good

thing you got here before Aunt Bayleigh drank all the coffee."

Bayleigh scowled. "Amie, must you be unpleasant?"

"Always," his sister answered without hesitation. "Mother, Johanna and Stone are adults. I believe they can manage to plan a small wedding on their own."

Bayleigh set her china cup aside. "Well, I imagine if they're not set on impressing anyone, that's just fine."

Amie's eyes narrowed. "Then Johanna and Stone will exceed your expectations."

Garnet cleared his throat and slid a hand along his wife's back.

"Forgive me, Amie." Bayleigh patted her daughter's knee before picking up her cup again. "I'm just getting antsy to plan a wedding for one of my children, but neither one of them shows signs of settling down. I hope you don't wait too long, daughter dear. Your biological clock is ticking."

"Mother, you surprise me. I thought you were concerned about me wrecking my figure." Amie's barb was unmistakable and there was no stopping the mother/daughter battle once it started rolling.

Bayleigh eyed her daughter over her coffee. "Amethyst, your pageant days are long past."

Alex's twin shot blue fire from her eyes at her mother. "Maybe I should look into a sperm donor."

Their father's mouth twitched, but he didn't look up from eating his food while reading his morning news on his tablet. "Don't rile your mother. The weekend's going to be long enough as it is."

Stone set down his fork long enough to say, "Alex has been seeing a single mother here with her son at HorsePower Cowkid Camp."

Alex grasped the change of subject with both hands, grateful to steer the conversation onto relatively safer ground—ground that wouldn't upset Gran. "Hey, cousin, that's no way to treat the man planning your bachelor party."

Not that he was really all that stoked about the party, which surprised the hell out of him. All he really wanted was to find Nina and Cody.

Amie laughed softly. "She would have figured it out soon enough anyway when you showed up at the rehearsal dinner with your redheaded bombshell in tow."

Alex shot his twin a glare. "You are not helping, Amie."

"A redhead." Bayleigh winced. "Well, if you have ginger children we can always fix that with a quick trip to the hair salon. Tell me more about her."

Alex didn't like the gleam in his mother's eyes one bit. Protective urges filled him. "Are those storm clouds overhead? Maybe we should move brunch inside."

His mother patted her hair. "Not even the threat of drenching will distract me from finding out more about this woman. You didn't answer my question, son."

"Mother." Alex leaned forward. "Her name is Nina and you *will* retract your claws and leave her alone. Don't pretend you don't know what I'm talking about. No interfering in my personal life. Period."

"Of course." Bayleigh pressed a hand to her chest with overplayed innocence. "I just want grandchildren. I dream of the days I can buy little smocked dresses or tiny cowboy boots."

"That subject is also off-limits," Alex said firmly. "As is your intent to choose their mother. I mean it."

His father looked up from his iPad for the first time. "This week's going to be interesting."

His grandmother's keen blue eyes took in all, and he hated that she'd witnessed the sparring, even if it was par for the course with their family gatherings. Alex wondered if maybe there was more to Gran's test than he'd originally thought. Could this be some sort of reverse psychology? Maybe she didn't want the stocks? Or had plans for another way to get them?

Could she be testing his honor to make sure none of his father's screwed-up values were running through him?

Damn, that stung.

He'd always been the different one, not a part of Diamonds in the Rough. But he'd thought his grandmother respected how he'd channeled his own work ethic and values into turning Hidden Gem into an asset to the empire and a tribute to their land.

Hell, he didn't know what to think right now. He just wanted to get this breakfast over with so he could spend time with Nina.

Rain pattered on the barn roof, and Nina cradled a cup of coffee with rich cream and two spoons of sugar. Sitting at a rustic picnic table in the café corner area, she'd been eating a pastry while watching her son. The children were scattered throughout the stalls that had been set up petting-zoo style. Each kid had been partnered with his or her choice of a pony, donkey, dog, chickens or even a rabbit to brush, hold or pet. Four stalls down, Cody ran a bristly brush along a miniature donkey, a teacher close at his side, instructing.

Nina wasn't needed now. Her son was enjoying independent play. She should be happy and go back to her cabin to read or nap with the rain soothing her to sleep. She'd certainly gotten very little sleep last night. She set down her coffee with a heavy sigh.

Her stomach had been in knots all day over the influx of McNairs and what that did—or didn't—mean in regards to her relationship with Alex. Whether making love or just talking, she'd enjoyed being alone with him. Solitude would be all but impossible now and she felt that she'd been robbed of her last few days left for a fling.

Except if it was just a fling, she shouldn't be this upset.

Thunder rolled outside, and Nina looked at her son quickly to make sure he wasn't upset. Some of the other children covered their ears, one squealed, but Cody was lost in the rhythmic stroking of the donkey's coat.

The barn door opened with a swirl of damp wind, and Alex ducked inside, closing the door quickly. He shook the rain off his hat, scanning the cavernous space. His eyes found hers in an instant and he smiled, his gaze steaming over her in a way that said he was thinking of last night too. She started to stand, but he waved for her to stay seated as he walked past her to her son.

Alex nodded to the teacher and let her angle away before taking the teacher's place beside Cody. Nina threw away her coffee and padded over silently, curious about what he intended to say.

And yes, eager to be near him.

Alex picked up a second brush, smoothing it over the donkey too. "I wasn't much of a talker either when I was younger," he said softly. "I know it's not quite the same as what's going on in your mind. But I wanted to let you know I understand that even when a person is quiet, he still hears. That's part of what I enjoy most about the animals here, in the quiet with them, it's easier to hear."

"Yes." Cody's little hand smoothed steadily. "My mommy broughted me here."

"You have a smart mommy. But I don't know you as well as your mom does. So, while I know you're listening, I can only guess what you would be interested in hearing. For all I know, I could be boring you talking about fishing when maybe you prefer soccer. It's okay for you to be quiet, but I would appreciate a hint on what you would like to talk about."

Cody set aside the brush and stroked the donkey's neck. "Donkey's nice."

"You like activities with horses, ponies, donkeys? You're okay with me talking about them?"

"Uh-huh." He kept rubbing the donkey without looking away.

"Okay, then. My cousin Stone has a quarter horse named Copper. My sister, Amie, has an Arabian named Crystal." He listed them in a way that Nina realized gave Cody a connection to each McNair. Since Cody loved the animals, he would have positive associations with the person. "My favorite is the Paint, named Zircon. My grandmother has this thing about naming every person and animal after a gemstone. She likes themes and patterns."

"I like patter-ins," Cody whispered, drawing the last word out so it had a third syllable.

"Okay, let's talk about the gem pattern names. People call me Alex, but my name is Alexandrite and my sister Amie is Amethyst. My grandmother even had dogs that had similar names."

"Dogs?" A spark lit in Cody's eyes and he tipped his head toward Alex. "Where are the dogs?"

"My grandmother is sick, so new families are taking care of three of the dogs. My cousin Stone has the fourth dog named Pearl, and my sister takes care of Gran's cats."

"Can I pet the doggy?"

Alex grinned. "How about puppies? Someone dropped a box of border collie mix puppies on our land a couple of weeks ago. They must have thought we would be a good home for them since one of our ranch hands has a border collie that works with him. Would you like to see the pups?"

Cody nodded quickly, eyes wide. "Uh-huh."

Nina's heart all but squeezed in two as Alex went out of his way to lead Cody to the pen of fuzzy border collie mix puppies tucked in the office. She stayed out of sight so as not to disrupt the moment. Two puppies played tug-of-war over a toy. Another flopped back over belly catching a ball, ears flopping. Alex showed her son different ways to play gently with the small fluff balls. Cody had such little time with male role models.

Alex made her ache and yearn for things she'd thought she could never have again. The ranch was well equipped for taking care of puppies and kittens who needed homes, and even helping struggling young moms and special-needs children, but she had to remember for her and for the puppies—Hidden Gem was a temporary stop. Only the McNairs stayed here. Like the puppies, Nina and Cody would be moving on to a different home and this place would be just a nostalgic memory.

An hour later, Nina took photos of her son riding a mechanical bull—with the bull set on a very slow speed to buck and turn. She could already envision one of these images reproduced onto a large canvas in her living room, surrounded by smaller photos from throughout this incredible week.

Would Alex be in any of those pictures? Could her heart take that kind of bittersweet reminder?

The rainstorm had ended a few minutes ago and since Cody was the last of the children to take a turn on the mechanical bull, the head camp counselor called out, "Line up, by your groups. Blue ponies here. Yellow ponies there. Green. And then red."

The children raced toward the door in a loose cluster, pent-up energy radiating off their little bodies. A girl in a wheelchair whizzed by, pumping the wheels faster and faster, pigtails flying.

Nina felt Alex's presence a second before he put his hand on her shoulder.

"Who are you sending the photos to?"

"A friend at home." She held up the cell phone. "Reed and I met at a support group for single parents with special-needs children."

"Reed?" His jaw flexed. "Should I be jealous of this guy?"

"No, we're just friends. Good friends who try to help each other, but we're only friends." She tucked away her phone before taking his hand, wishing she could do more. But anyone could walk in, and children were within eyesight. "I wouldn't have been with you this week if there was someone else."

"Good, I'm glad to hear that." His thumb slid around to stroke the inside of her wrist. "Did you get your turn on the mechanical bull?"

She blinked in surprise. "Um, no. That activity was just for the kids."

"I own it." He patted the saddle. "Do you want to try?"

"I'm not going to put on some *Urban Cowboy* sexy ride show for you."

He grinned, a roguish twinkle in his blue eyes. "I wasn't proposing anything of the sort—especially not with kids nearby. But even the mention is filling my mind with interesting ideas." He squeezed her hand. "For now, how about a regular slow ride?"

Somehow he made even that sound sensual. Irresistible. She approached the mechanical bull tentatively, touching the saddle.

Alex's hand fell to rest on her shoulder. "There are different speeds. We take this as slow as you want to go."

She glanced back at him. "Are we still talking about the bull?"

"Do you want us to talk about something else?"

Her stomach flipped and she looked away. "I guess I'm riding the bull."

"All right, then. Climb on. Grab hold and we'll start her slow."

"Okay, but no pictures." She stepped into the stirrup and swung her leg over, sitting, half sliding off the other side before righting herself with a laugh. "I never was much of one for carnival rides."

"Let me know if you want to stop." He turned the knob, setting the bull into a gentle rocking motion that started to turn.

"I tossed my cookies once on the Ferris wheel," she confessed as the bull circled.

"I know where the mop is."

"An almighty McNair mops floors?" she teased, trying not to think about the day they'd ridden the horse together.

He increased the speed. "Gran brought us up with down-home, work-ethic values. We had jobs on the farm as kids and teenagers, just like everyone else, and we had to start at the bottom, learning every stage of the operation."

She gripped tighter. "What did your parents have to say about that?"

"Not much as long as the big money kept flowing their way."

"Your father didn't work?" That seemed so atypical compared to what she'd seen from Alex working up a sweat on the ranch in addition to his desk work running the place.

"My father has an office. He makes business trips, but does he work? Not really. I guess Gran wanted to make doubly sure the grandkids turned out differently. And we did. Although we always thought Stone would run the company, he decided to run a nonprofit camp instead."

She read rumors of a new CEO outside the family being hired to run Diamonds in the Rough, but she hadn't paid more than passing attention. "That must have been a huge disappointment to your grandmother not to be able to pass along her legacy to her children."

"It was—and is. But she's happy about the camp. Who wouldn't be proud of this? It's amazing, innovative and rewarding. I just want her to be at peace in her final days." Shadows chased through his blue eyes.

"All that parents want is for their children to be happy and try their best."

His eyes met hers. "Not all parents."

"Are you saying your grandmother—"

"Not my grandmother. My parents." Looking down, he scuffed his boots through the dirt. "Let's talk about something else. Like how's that bull feeling? Ready to take him up a notch? If you can still talk, it's obviously not going fast enough."

She shook her head quickly. "I think it's time to stop."

He switched off the controls and the bull slowed, slowed and finally went still. Alex reached up to help her down. "I'm going to miss you tonight while I'm at the bachelor party."

She slid down the front of him, enjoying the feel of their bodies against each other, her mind firing with memories from the night before. "I thought men lived for those sorts of things."

"I would rather be with you tonight." His warm breath caressed her neck.

She pressed her cheek to his heart for just a moment, listening to the steady thud. "That's really sweet of you to say."

"My thoughts are far from sweet." He growled softly in her ear, "I'd love to see you after the party if it's not too late."

His words rang with an unmistakable promise and she didn't have the least inclination to say no.

Nine

Alex knew he was in trouble when he couldn't stop checking his watch for the end of the bachelor party. He wanted to spend the evening with Nina and Cody. But he owed Stone this traditional testosterone bash. Stone was more like a brother to him than a cousin, so for now, thoughts of Nina and her son needed to take a backseat.

The party was being held in a private lodge behind the Hidden Gem ranch house. Cigar smoke filled the room along with round poker tables. A buffet full of food and a bar stocked with the best alcohol and brews stayed stocked throughout the night. Country music piped through the sound system, a steel guitar still audible over raucous laughter, the clink of glasses and the whirr of a few electric card shufflers at work.

Garnet, Stone and Preston Armstrong, the new company CEO, sat with Alex at one table. Four more tables held longtime employees from the Diamonds in the Rough Jewelry and the Hidden Gem Ranch. Stone had insisted on the bachelor party being held the day before the rehearsal dinner, not wanting any of his friends to be nursing hangovers at his wedding.

Preston threw his cards down, gray eyes tired from concentration. "Fold. This is the lamest bachelor party ever."

Alex laughed, tossing turquoise and white chips into the middle of the table. The chips clinked and fell haphazardly in a pile. "You're just pissed because you're not winning."

"You could have a point there," Preston conceded, shoulders sagging.

Stone passed new cards to the remaining players. "My orders for the evening. Nothing but booze and cards."

"Not even a movie?"

Stone grinned devilishly. "Haven't you heard? I'm saving myself for marriage."

"Yeah, well, what about the rest of us?" Preston barked.

Stone shrugged, finishing his drink. He rattled the leftover ice in his glance. "Have your own bachelor party, and you get to make your own rules."

"Not going to happen," Preston insisted, palms up as he pushed back from the table. "While y'all finish this hand, I'll use the time to become reacquainted with the bar."

Garnet tossed in his hand. "I'm out too. Another drink sounds good."

Alex looked at the two pairs in his hand and slid a few more chips to the middle of the table. "I'm happy for you and Johanna." He paused to look at his cousin across the table. "I hope you know I mean that."

"That's good to hear," Stone answered, his voice hoarse with emotion. Stone's features flattened as he stared at the pile of chips, avoiding Alex's gaze. "You mean as much to me as any brother ever could."

"I'm sorry it even had to be said. She and I were too much alike to ever be a couple. Any feelings I thought I felt were more habit than anything else."

Because Alex knew now that anything he'd thought he felt for Johanna paled in comparison to what he felt for Nina.

"Well, loving a woman is rarely easy." Stone peeled his eyes up toward Alex.

Alex rubbed the cards in his hand. The plastic of the cards hummed, seeming to drown out all the other sounds of the bachelor party. "I'm learning that."

Stone set his cards facedown. "The mom with her son here at the camp?"

"Forget I said anything. And for God's sake, don't let anybody say anything more to my mother." Alex tipped back his drink. While it looked as though he had been slamming back vodka all night, his drinks had all been water. He wanted a clear head for later. He wanted to enjoy Nina. Their time together was short and he didn't need a single sense dulled. "This is about you tonight, cousin."

Stone pushed his cards into the middle. "Well, damn, then let's bail and go riding. You and me, like old times."

Now, that sounded a helluva lot more appealing than sitting here. Alex scraped his chair back, but had to ask, "Is it fair to leave Preston stuck with my father?"

"Preston's the boss now." Stone stood, his smile widening. "That's the beauty of having found my own path, cousin. Johanna and I answer only to ourselves and each other."

"Good point."

They clinked glasses, drained the contents and left the party. And Alex couldn't help thinking how damn important family was to him.

Even more important than the ranch? Or were they inextricable? Hell, if he knew the answer.

Stone and Alex hadn't been on a night ride in years. When they were kids, they used to steal away, ride deep into the night to get away from their respective parents. There was something calming in taking to the trails together, even if they didn't speak a helluva lot to each other.

Alex glanced over at his cousin. "Are you ready?"

Stone was preparing to mount Copper, his sorrel quarter horse.

"I bet you I can still whup your ass from here to the creek," Stone said, steadying himself on Copper. He tightened the reins, creating a curved arch in Copper's neck. The horse was sheer power.

The quarter horse danced with anticipation, sock-covered legs shifting from side to side, issuing a challenge.

"I doubt that. You're rusty these days." Alex absently stroked Zircon's neck. Zircon turned his head to nuzzle Alex's knee.

"It is my bachelor party, you know," Stone said dryly.

Alex smiled lazily. "All right. On my mark, though."

Stone nodded, urging Copper next to Zircon.

"One. Two. Three. Go."

Zircon leaped forward, seeming to read Alex's thoughts. That was what had always made horses easy for him. The nonverbal communication. The unexplainable connection.

From the corner of his vision, he could see the glint of Copper's tack. Stone was a stride ahead of him. Collecting his reins, Alex opened up Zircon's pace.

Zircon's ears pinned back as the horse surged forward. Finally Alex gained on his cousin as they drew closer to the creek. Memories of riding with Nina, of kissing her out here in the open on McNair land filled him. He had to see her tonight. No matter how late. Even if just to slide into bed with her and listen to her sleep.

The sensation of the gallop reverberated through Alex's bones. Shaking his thigh. Wait. The buzz wasn't from the connection of hooves and ground. It was his cell phone vibrating. *Damn.*

"Stone," he called out. "Hold on. Someone's calling."

As Alex slowed Zircon to a walk, the familiar ringtone replaced the hammering of hooves. Amie's ringtone. Amie who never called this late at night unless it was important. Or if there was trouble.

Hands shaking, Alex retrieved the phone from his pants. Stone slowed Copper, his face knotting with concern.

Alex took a deep breath. "Hello?"

Amie's voice pierced through the receiver. "It's Gran. She's got a horrible headache and the nurse is concerned. You know Gran never complains. We have to take her to the emergency room. It's faster than calling an ambulance. Please, you have to get here. Now."

"Stone and I will be right there." Alex looked at his cousin. "We've got to get to Gran. Something's wrong."

Stone nodded, his jaw tight with worry. Both men turned their horses back toward the barn. This time, they raced for another reason. For family. And Alex could swear Zircon burst quicker than he ever had before.

While she waited for Alex, Nina stretched out in her bed reading a Spanish translation of an American romance novel, work and pleasure all at once. She'd quickly become accustomed to having adult conversation at night and missed him.

And yes, her body burned to be with him again.

She glanced at her cell phone resting on top of the quilt. He'd said he would text when he was on his way so he wouldn't startle her. He was always so thoughtful, and the way he understood Cody made it tougher than ever to think about the end of the week. A lot could happen in the next few days.

Look how much already had.

Her cell phone vibrated on the bed—she'd been afraid to keep the ringer on for fear of waking up Cody. She scooped up her cell and found an incoming text. From Alex.

Delayed. Gran has severe headache. Going to ER.

Nina's fingers clenched around the phone, her heart aching for him. She texted back quickly.

So sorry. Prayers for your grandmother.

She wished she could do more, say more, have the right to go with him and comfort him. It was obvious his grandmother was like a mom to him. He spoke so highly of her and clearly admired her. Alex had to be going through a lot. How amazing that he still had so much to give both her and Cody this week between the wedding, his work and his grandmother's declining health.

Nina clutched the phone to her chest, flopping over to her back to watch the ceiling fan blades swirl. Had she been wrong to cut herself off from dating for so long? Did she even know how to answer that question when she couldn't even imagine being with any man other than Alex?

This was becoming such a tangle so fast when she'd been determined to never again to make an impulsive decision, to allow herself to be swept off her feet.

The phone hummed again and she pulled it up fast, elbowing to sit up. Hoping that it was Alex with good news.

Except it was an incoming call from her friend. "Hello, Reed."

"Hope I'm not calling too late."

"Not at all. I'm just reading, feeling lazy." She turned off the e-reader and set it on the bedside table. "Is everything okay at home?"

"I had to call. Those photos of Cody are incredible." Reed's favored eighties radio station played in the background. "I'm signing Wendy up. They had to put her on the waiting list, though. You sure were lucky to get a slot."

Nina thought back to her flurry of packing and preparation when the surprise slot and discount fee came open so quickly. "They told me there was a last-minute cancellation."

"And a waiting list a mile long."

She sat up straighter. "I don't know how to explain it, but I can put in a good word for you with the McNairs. I've, uh, gotten to know them this week."

"That would be fabulous, sweetie. Thanks. I wouldn't ask for myself, but it's for Wendy." He paused. "You're doing okay, then?"

"Cody's thriving. I'm doing great, enjoying the change of scenery." She used to travel often with her UN job. She missed that sometimes, and that made her feel guilty. It wasn't Cody's fault. The support group where she'd met Reed and learned to cope had changed her life and saved her sanity. "Wendy will love it here and so will you."

"Glad to hear it. Well, keep those photos coming. Night."

"Night," she responded, disconnecting and flopping back again. Her thoughts swirled and she felt she was missing something in her exhaustion.

She couldn't account for how she'd gotten the slot this week, but she knew everything about meeting Alex McNair felt as though it was meant to be, each day more perfect than the last. She was tired of being wary and cautious. Her time with Alex had been a personal fairy tale and she wasn't willing to question that. He was different than her frog-prince ex-husband. Alex had to be.

Sleep tugged at her and maybe a bit of denial too, because she just wanted to enjoy her remaining days here and let the future wait.

With only the moonlight in his bedroom to guide him, Alex tugged off his shirt, which still held the scent of smoke from the bachelor party and a hint of the anti-

septic air from the hospital. The ER doc had diagnosed
Gran with dehydration. An IV bag of fluid later, they'd
released her to come home under the care of her nurse.

Or rather she'd insisted nothing would keep her from
making the most of the wedding weekend with her family. She would check with her doctor every day and
she already had round-the-clock nurses staying at the
house. But she was dying and no amount of meds would
change that.

Anger and denial roared through him. He didn't want
to stay here and he didn't feel like sleeping. He yanked
a well-worn green T-shirt from the drawer and tugged it
over his head. The grandfather clock in his suite chimed
three times in the dark. Regardless of the time, he had
to see Nina.

He opened the doors out to his patio, leaped over the
railing and jogged across the lawn toward her cabin. He
had a key. She'd given him one for tonight right before
he left. The full moon shot rays through the oak trees,
along the path. Most of the cabins were dark. The only
sounds were bugs and frogs. He took the steps up to
Nina's two at a time and let himself inside quietly.

He checked on Cody first. A buckaroo bronco lamp
glowed on the dresser. The boy slept deeply, his blond
hair shiny in the soft light, his room cool and his weighted
blanket on top of him. Nina had told Alex once that the
cocooned feeling helped her son with serotonin production or something like that he'd meant to read up on.

He closed the door carefully and stepped into Nina's
room. She was beautiful, princesslike even. Her bold
red curls piled around her neck. Causal. Desirable. She
was asleep on top of the covers, her cell phone in her
left hand and her e-reader on the bedside table. She had

on a light pink *C'est La Vie* T-shirt with a picture of the Eiffel Tower. The shirt barely covered her thighs. He thought about taking her there. To Paris. To Rome. And so many other places. To bed.

If she could forgive him for his half-truths this week.

Sitting on the edge, he eased the covers back. "Nina, it's me."

"Alex," she sighed, her voice groggy as she rolled toward him to portion of the bed with the quilt pushed aside. "How's your grandmother?"

Her concern was apparent, even if she wasn't fully awake. Damn.

"Gran is at home resting peacefully in her own bed. She was just dehydrated from the summer heat." He tugged the covers over Nina, kicked off his shoes and slid into bed beside her. "I hope you don't mind that I'm here. I know it's late, but I missed you."

"So glad you came." She cuddled closer, her arm sliding around his waist. "Missed you too."

Her warm soft body fit against his, the sweet smell of her shampoo filling every breath. He stroked her back in lazy circles, taking comfort in touching her. Hell, just being with her. His body throbbed in response, but she was asleep. So he gritted his teeth and tried to will away the erection.

Easier said than done.

She wriggled closer with a sleepy sigh. He bit back a groan. Maybe coming here and expecting he could just sleep hadn't been such a wise idea after all.

Her leg nestled between his. The soft skin of her calf added fuel to his already flaming fire. He ached to be inside her, to hear those kittenish sighs of pleasure mixed with demands for more. She was a passionate, giving lover. He wondered what it would have been like if her last name wasn't Lowery and she'd just been a regular mom bringing her son to camp.

She slid her hand down his side over his hip, wriggling against him. Was she dreaming? The thought of her having sensual dreams turned him inside out. But he couldn't take advantage of her that way.

Then her hand slipped around to cradle his erection.

He grasped her wrist and willed himself to move away. "Nina, you're dreaming."

Her eyelashes swept up and she smiled at him. "Dreaming? Not hardly."

Her voice was groggy, although she was very obviously awake. She unzipped his pants and wrapped her fingers around the length of him. His eyes slid closed and he allowed himself a moment to enjoy the sensation of her touch. The outside world would be intruding soon enough. This could well be his last chance alone with her before she dumped him—or his family scared her away.

"Nina..." he groaned, his arms going around her as he rolled to tuck her beneath him. "I need you."

"How perfectly convenient," she murmured in a husky voice, "because I've been dreaming of you and I need you too. Now. Inside me. I've been thinking about you all night long."

He fished out his wallet and tossed a condom on the bed before sweeping her underwear down. She kicked them aside with an efficient flick. And his whole body shouted to thrust inside her. But he needed to imprint himself in her memory—her in his own—in case this was their last time together.

No. It couldn't be their last night together. He refused to entertain the possibility.

He kissed along her jaw, her neck, then lower, between her breasts and lower still. Her breath hitched as she picked up his intent seconds before he nuzzled between her legs. He blew a light puff of air over her and she shivered, her fingers sliding into his hair, tugging lightly. She arched up as he stroked and laved. Each purr and moan and sigh from her had him throbbing with the need to take her. Her head thrashed back and forth on her pillow, her pleasure so beautiful to watch.

Then she tugged at his shoulders, scratching, urging him breathlessly, "So close. I want to come with you inside me, but I can't hold out much longer."

He didn't need to be told again. Pressing a final intimate kiss to her, he slid back up her body, nipping along her stomach and her breasts. Her hands impatient, she took the weight of him in her palms stroking, coaxing until he growled in frustration.

Smiling with feminine power, she sheathed him with another arousing stroke. He covered her, settling between her thighs, waiting even though holding back was pure torture. Finally she opened her eyes and looked straight at him. Holding her gaze, he pushed inside her velvety warmth with a powerful thrust. And damn, he was glad she was near her own release, because his was only a few strokes away. He moved inside her, again and again, her legs wrapping around his waist, drawing him deeper.

The bed creaked and the ceiling fan blew cool gusts over his back. But even blasts from the air conditioner couldn't stop the heat pumping through his veins. He saw the flush of impending release climbing up her neck, and he captured her mouth, taking her cries of completion, his own mixing with hers.

Perfection. Nina. Coming undone in his arms.

Rolling to his side, he held her to him, the aftershocks rippling through them. The night sounds of bugs and frogs sounded along with a gentle patter of a rain shower starting up again. He smoothed his hand over her hair, her face tucked against his chest until eventually her breathing returned to normal, then slower as sleep grabbed hold of her again.

So much weighed on his heart—between his grandmother's illness and the impossible position she'd put him in. He couldn't wait another day to unburden himself, even if he knew Nina was sleeping. And yeah, maybe he also needed to test out the words to find a way to tell her when the time was right. "Nina, I need to tell you something."

"Mmm," she answered, her eyes closed. Her arm draped limply over him.

He knew she likely couldn't hear, but still he confessed everything his grandmother had asked him to do, how torn he felt, how much he wanted her... And the unheard words didn't make him feel any better. So he just held her until the sun started to peek from the horizon. He needed to leave before her son woke. Alex had to prepare for his cousin's rehearsal dinner.

And for the proverbial storm that his mother brought to every occasion.

Nerves made Nina restless about her date with Alex. Her hand shook as she swept on mascara, leaning toward the mirror and praying she wouldn't end up looking like a clown this evening. She had tried out a makeup tutorial from the internet to update her look since she didn't get out much these days. Winged eyeliner. Classy and timeless but she would have to watch the sweat this weekend.

It was only a date. She was just Alex's plus-one for his cousin's rehearsal dinner. Except it wasn't just any party. It was a McNair affair, an exclusive event.

And Nina was sleeping with him. They'd gone beyond a one-night fling. And he'd left her the sweetest note on her pillow, in Spanish this time. Not perfect, but perfectly adorable. He'd complemented her beauty while sleeping and said she would be in his thoughts all day. She'd already tucked the note into her suitcase along with the card he'd given her with the wildflowers.

So yes, she wanted to be at her best and only had the limited wardrobe she'd packed for a children's cowboy camp.

She'd taken two hours this morning to race around and find new dresses to wear to the rehearsal party and the wedding, and an outfit for Cody tomorrow. She'd thought she misheard Alex when he said he wanted her son to attend the wedding, and she was more than a little nervous for her child. But Alex assured her it would be a casual affair with a Texas flair Cody would enjoy. There would even be three other children there.

It was almost as if she belonged here. With Alex.

A dangerous thought. They'd only known each other a few days. But she damn sure intended to leave an indelible impression on his memory.

She clipped on a brass bracelet with Spanish inscriptions, another acquisition from Diamonds in the Rough, and smoothed her loose chevron-patterned sundress. She admired her freshly painted toenails peeking out of her strappy sandals and stepped out of her bedroom into the living room, then stopped short, her heart squeezing at the sight in front of her. Alex and her son, both catnapping.

Cody curled up on the sofa, hugging his blanket and wearing new puppy dog pj's she'd picked up for him during her shopping spree this morning. The actual wedding rehearsal had already taken place and she'd skipped that to prepare her son before Alex came by to pick her up.

Alex snored softly in the fat leather chair, his booted feet propped on the ottoman. Her gaze skated from his boots, up muscular legs in khakis, past a Diamonds in the Rough belt buckle, to broad shoulders in a sports coat. A Stetson covered his face. He looked so much like his cousin Stone it would have been easy for someone to mistake the two men for each other. But she would know her man anywhere.

Her man?

When had she started thinking in possessive terms like that? And after such a short time knowing him?

They'd stolen late-night dates, but his days had been taken up with work and she'd focused on Cody's camp—other than keeping her cell phone in reach at all times, treasuring each quick call or text from Alex.

Oh God, she was in serious trouble here.

He tapped his hat upward and he whistled softly. "Nice!"

"Thanks," she said, spinning, the skirt rustling along her knees, "I guess it's time?"

"The sitter is already warming Cody's supper in the kitchen." Standing, Alex walked toward her, eyes stroking her the whole way. "And I queued up his favorite videos, since he'll probably be up late because he napped."

She stepped into the circle of his arms. "Is there anything you haven't thought of?"

"I sure hope not. I'm doing everything in my power to ensure that this evening is as pleasant as possible to make up for having to spend time with my mother."

"She can't be that bad." Certainly not as bad as Nina's in-laws. They'd been distant while she was married, but grew outright hostile after her divorce. And now? They barely acknowledged Cody existed. They rarely spoke to her. "I'll be fine."

He squeezed her arm. "Okay, then. But if you need me to rescue you from her, give me a sign. Like tug on your earlobe."

Laughing, she hooked arms with him, then ducked her head in to say hello to the sitter before they left. One of the camp counselors had agreed to watch Cody.

After a short walk to the open air barn full of family and friends, Nina found herself searching for his parents. Curious after all she'd heard. Alex went straight for them as if to get past the introductions and move on. An older couple stood together under an oak tree strung with white lights. The pair was easily identifiable as his parents by the resemblance. Although their idea of casual sure came with a lot of starch and spray tan.

"Mother, Dad," Alex said, placing a possessive hand on Nina's back, "this is Nina Lowery."

Bayleigh McNair was a beautiful woman, no question—except for her beady eyes, which moved around quickly, assessing without ever meeting Nina's gaze. "Lovely to meet you, dear. How long have you and my son been seeing each other?"

"Mom, I already told you she's here with her son for Stone's new camp." His hand twitched ever so slightly, even though his voice stayed amiable.

"So you just met this week." Eyebrows raised, Bayleigh looked at Nina as if she were a gold digger.

Indignation fired hot and fierce. How unfair and judgmental. And Nina had no choice but to keep her mouth closed and be polite. "We met my first day here. I thought he was one of the ranch hands. Can you imagine that?"

"How quaint." Bayleigh half smiled.

Amie joined them, the feathers on her skirt brushing Nina's legs. "Mother, you're being rude. Stop it or I'll wear white shoes after Labor Day."

Her mother sniffed, looking offended. "No need to be obnoxious, dear."

Alex's father folded her hand in his. "Nina, it's lovely to meet you. And your last name, Lowery... If I remember correctly, you married into the Lowery Resort family."

"Yes, sir." She shook his hand briskly, then twined her fingers in front of her. She wasn't comfortable talking about money the way these people were. That was her son's money, her ex-husband's wealth. She'd grown up in a regular middle-class neighborhood.

Garnet clapped his son on the shoulder. "That's mighty big of you, son, letting the competition in here this way."

Nina frowned. "Competition?"

Bayleigh swatted her husband's arm. "Leave the poor girl alone before Amie threatens us again. You heard Alex say she's here with her child, you know, for that *special* camp. For *special* kids."

Nina bristled. That last comment went too far. Digs at her were one thing. But her son was off-limits. Was this woman that clueless or deliberately baiting her?

Alex's father hooked arms with his wife to steer her away—thank heavens. "We should check on Mother. Inside."

Bayleigh patted his hand. "I know it's so hard for you to see her that way."

Garnet's chin trembled and he leaned on his wife. Amie cursed softly and walked into the barn full of tables and a dais.

Alex's jaw flexed and he hung his head, sweeping his hat off to scratch a hand through his hair. "I am so damn sorry for my mother's behavior. It's inexcusable." He dropped his hat back on his head. "I wouldn't blame you if you wanted to leave now."

Nina rocked on her heels. "I have to confess, she's a lot to take in all at once, but I'm fine. There's plenty to celebrate here and other people to meet. Let's have fun."

"That's diplomatic and kind of you." He caressed her shoulders, comforting and arousing at the same time. "Is there something I can do other than gag my parents?"

As angry as his mother had made her, Nina could let it go. The woman was superficial and catty. However, Nina's mind was quietly turning over the "competition" thing Alex's father had mentioned. What had she missed? She thought about how Reed had insisted spots at this camp were impossible to come by. Had someone in the McNair organization wanted to keep the competition close?

Certainly there was no way Alex would know about her relation to the Lowerys, was there? She shook off the suspicion.

Alex was clearly hurting now over his mom's behavior, and it wasn't fair to blame him for his mother or take out her frustration on him. "I know your parents are grieving too. People are rarely at their best when they're hurting."

His hands slid up to cup her face. "That's more generous than she deserves. More generous than I deserve too, because I should have given you a stronger warning."

"You're not responsible for your parents." Now that her anger had faded to a low simmer, she saw the pain they'd caused him. "Are *you* okay?"

He folded her hand in his. "I'm a big boy. I know my parents. I just want better for Gran, especially now."

"Your grandmother *has* better. She has *you*." Nina took in the angles of his face, touched by the wind and sun, nothing affected or fake. "And she has Amie—I like your sister."

His mouth twitched. "She's a character."

"From everything I've seen of Stone and his fiancée, they've made your grandmother very happy with their wedding. And I assume seeing you there with a date on your arm will reassure her, as well." Another suspicion blindsided her, one she hadn't considered. "Is that why you've been pursuing me? To make your grandmother happy by having a date at the wedding?"

He hesitated, then shook his head. "I'm not sleeping with you to make my grandmother happy." His throat moved in a long swallow. "But there is something important I need to tell you once we're alone."

Ten

The three hours since Alex had said they needed to talk had passed at a torturous snail's pace. Nina wondered how much longer she could hold out waiting to hear what Alex needed to tell her. Good or bad? But if it had been good, wouldn't he have told her right then?

Her mind raced with darker possibilities. Had she allowed herself to get too excited over him? Overanalyzed his gestures? Made too much out of a few days?

She swiped sweat from her brow, searching for the restroom to make sure her mascara and eyeliner hadn't dripped into raccoon eyes after all the dancing she'd done. The live country band had started their first set with a Garth Brooks classic and Nina had thrown herself into the fun with both feet, telling herself to enjoy every moment she could before her time with Alex ended. She'd had fun, but after almost an hour on the dance floor, Nina was certain she looked like a train wreck.

She slid around tables full of guests enjoying after-dinner drinks and coffee. The desserts were all shaped and decorated like jewels. The event was lavish but personal, and touching, reminding her of all she'd once dreamed of having when she started her life with Warren.

Her imagination had been running wild all evening through dinner. Coveted camp slots? Lowerys competing with McNairs? A grandmother who wanted to see her grandchildren settled before she died.

Nina's instincts shouted that something was off, but she couldn't figure out exactly how she fit into the picture. And this wasn't the first time Alex had said he wanted to talk to her. Her heart beat faster, her chest going tight.

She tugged open a door and instead of a bathroom she found an office, with a desk, chairs—and Amie sprawled on the rust-colored velvet sofa. Her eyes were closed, but she was clearly awake. Tear tracks streaked through her makeup.

Nina stepped into the room and closed the door quickly behind her. "Amie?" she asked, walking to the sofa. "What's wrong? Are you all right?"

"Hell no." She peeked out of one eye, dragging in deep breaths. "But I will be."

Kneeling, Nina touched her arm. "Is there something I can do? Get you a tissue? A drink?"

"How about a pair of lead shoes, preferably men's size twelve?" Amie said bitterly, sitting upright and swinging her feet to the floor, tucking her feet back into her high heels.

"Ouch. Sounds bad." Sounded man-bad.

"Nothing I can't handle. I'm usually better at controlling my emotions, but there's so much going on…" She eyed the dartboard, strode over with determination and grabbed a handful of darts from the tray and plucked three from the target. "Next best thing to lead shoes? A dart, right in the face."

Nina winced. "Um, I'm not sure that's legal."

Amie backed away from the board. "I'm not going to stab him literally. Just imagine his face right there…" She lined up the toss. "…Bull's-eye. Every time. Rage does funny things like that."

"Remind me never to make you mad." Nina raised her hands in surrender, offering Amie a playful smile.

"Ah, honey." Amie turned fast and gave Nina a hard hug, one of the darts in Amie's fist scratching a little against Nina's back. "I would never hurt you. You're too nice."

"Do you mind if I ask which man made you mad? Family?" She saw a no and finished, "Or someone else?"

"Someone—" Amie pitched a dart "—else." She launched another.

"I'm sorry. I know how much it hurts to be betrayed by a man." Nina's ex-husband had left a river of pain in his wake, one she was still fording.

Amie avoided Nina's eyes, charged up to the board and pulled out the darts one at a time. "You're a strong, beautiful woman. Don't let anyone in my family walk over you."

Nina's nerves gathered into a big knot of uncertainty about Alex's secret. She churned over a million possibilities, but regardless of which one was true, they all led to the same ending.

Alex was going to break things off with her. Of course he was. He'd clearly just needed a date for the night. He had something to prove to his mother. To Johanna. Nina was just arm candy.

She'd wanted a fling, and Lord, she'd gotten it. This one week and one week only. And it was over. Her stomach plummeted worse than when Zircon had spooked.

What a time to realize she wanted more. What a time to realize how easy it would have been to have a life here with Alex.

Alex guided Nina out onto the dance floor, having ached to have her in his arms all night long. He had feelings for her that were about more than sex. He cared about her. Admired her even.

And he had to be honest with her, even if that cost him the ranch. He wanted his grandmother to be happy, but he couldn't do that at the expense of his honor. Seeing the strength and commitment—and love—Nina showered on her son made Alex realize he needed to man up.

"Let's dance outside, where it's less crowded," he said, clasping her hand and steering her into a dance under the lit oak trees.

The night was beautiful, the air cooler and the music a little quieter outdoors. Two people sat on a bench talking, and another couple danced, but none of them were close enough to overhear.

She was stiff in his arms, reserved and dodging his gaze. His mother had clearly done damage as usual. God, where did he even start?

"Nina—"

"Go ahead," she blurted out, her legs brushing against his.

He paused, angling back to look into her eyes. "Go ahead and what?"

"Go ahead and break things off with me. That's what you wanted to tell me, isn't it?" she asked, her face void of expression. She'd already built a tall wall between them. "You don't have to make this any more awkward than it already is. We had a fling and it's over. You don't need me to be your plus one at the wedding tomorrow. Dance with your sister, enjoy your family."

He pressed his fingers to her mouth. "That's not what I wanted to say at all."

A flicker of uncertainty sparked in her green eyes. Something that looked like cautious hope. "Then what is it?"

"I owe you an apology for not being up front at the start."

"I thought we discussed that already. You hid the fact that you weren't just a ranch hand. But we moved past that." Her fingers clenched, bunching his shirt in her hands. "It was a minor misunderstanding."

This was tougher than he'd expected but long overdue. "When my grandmother's cancer was first diagnosed, stock prices dropped because of concerns about the future of the holdings. My cousin and my grandmother thought they'd tracked the purchasers of those stocks to make sure no one group amassed a portion large enough to risk gaining control of the company."

Her eyes went from wary to resigned. "Something went wrong."

"Lowery Resorts has been buying up McNair stocks."

Her feet stopped moving altogether. His words hung between them, his gut heavy with guilt.

"My in-laws." Her hands fell to her sides; her fists clenched.

"In a sense. Your son's trust fund uses the same investment broker. He used shell corporations to buy up stocks for your son as well as your in-laws. The stocks that went to your son slipped under our radar."

"Until now." She sagged to sit on a rustic wooden bench. "It's no accident that I'm here, is it?"

He sat beside her, his hands clasped between his knees. "No, my grandmother made sure you received the brochure and the scholarship."

She met his gaze full on, her chin set but her eyes glistening with unshed tears. "And your role in this?"

"My grandmother wants me to encourage you to sell those stocks back to us."

Her eyebrows pinched together. Her face was impassive. The wall from earlier sprang back in full force. Damn. "Why didn't you just say that from the start? We could have negotiated."

"We didn't think you would agree." How had this ever made sense to him? He should have known this was a train wreck in the making from the start. He should have passed it over to the lawyers and accountants and let them handle it. Emotions screwed up business. "It's a great time to buy but not a good time to sell. In all honesty, it wouldn't be in your son's best interest to sell."

"Why is there an issue with having other stockholders?"

"Think about the resorts your in-laws build and look at Hidden Gem." The thought of his home being turned into a tourist trap made him ill. "We have a problem."

"More than one apparently." Sighing, she blinked fast and slumped back against the bench. Her mouth opened slightly, allowing a breath of words to escape. "How much of what we shared was even real, Alex?"

"God, Nina, how can you even ask that? My grandmother not only wanted me to persuade you to give up those stocks, but she led me to believe my inheritance depended on it, like a test to prove how badly I wanted my piece of the family business. But I couldn't do what she asked. I pursued you in spite of her test. I'm being honest with you now. I never wanted those stocks to come between us." He reached for her only to have her flinch away. His worst nightmare come true. He'd told her the truth and she hated him for it. Not that he could blame her. It sounded awful when he laid it out. If he could only make her see he cared about her. About her kid. It wasn't about the stocks anymore. It never had been. He was falling for her and her son.

Footsteps sounded behind him, and Nina looked over his shoulder, distracted. He glanced back to find his sister racing toward them, a ringing purse in her hand.

"Nina, you left your bag back on the sofa. The sitter has been trying to reach you. She called me too."

Nina shot to her feet, her eyes wide with alarm. "Did Cody wake up? I need to go to him."

Alex knew his sister well, and even though she appeared poised, he could see the signs of blind panic. Something was wrong, very wrong. He stood beside Nina.

Amie clasped Nina's hands. "No, it's not that. I'm sorry to have to tell you this, but Cody is missing."

Alex's nightmare just got a whole lot worse.

"Cody!" Nina shouted into the night, her voice hoarse, her heart raw. Holding a flashlight, she walked alongside Alex into woods.

The staff was checking every inch of the lodge and the cabins. The family and guests were searching the grounds. She was running on fumes and fear. Other voices echoed in the distance shouting her son's name, but she knew too well even if he heard, he very well might not be able to open up enough to answer.

Her world was collapsing. Her son had wandered off. The sitter had put him to bed, and she was positive he hadn't gone out past her. His window was open. And he was gone.

Nina had been frantic and tried to bolt out to begin searching, but Alex had remained calm, held her back and reminded her that an organized approach would cover more ground faster. Ranch security had been notified and a grid search was under way.

Knowing that everything possible was being done hadn't made the last hour any less horrific. She'd allowed herself to be charmed and distracted by a man who was only using her, and now her child was in danger. She would never forgive herself. Served her right for believing she was in another fairy tale.

Alex swept his larger spotlight across the path leading to the creek they'd once soared over on a horseback. Nausea roiled. The thought of her son drowning…

She bit back a whimper.

Sweeping the spotlight along the creek, Alex stepped over a log. "We'll find him. We have plans in place for things like this, grid searches and manpower. We'll find him before you know it."

"This is my fault." And there was nothing anyone could say to convince her otherwise. She walked alongside the water, shallow, probably not deep enough to be a worry, but everywhere was dangerous to a boy with little understanding of fears or boundaries. "I should have been with him tonight."

"It's impossible for you to be with him every minute of every day," Alex pointed out logically. "The sitter has excellent credentials too."

And yes, he was right. But that meant nothing to a mother in the grip of her worst nightmare. "That's not making me feel any better."

"This kind of thing happens even when there's a houseful of adults watching." His spotlight swept over a trickling waterfall, no sign of her son. "You can't be attached at the hip."

"Intellectually I know that. But in my heart? I'll never forgive myself."

A rustling in the woods drew her up short. She struggled to listen, to discern…A rabbit leaped out of the brush and scampered away. Disappointment threatened to send her to her knees. Alex's arm slid around her to bolster her.

She drew in a shaky breath and regained her footing. "You can relax. I'm not planning to sue the camp. I just want to find my son."

"Nina, God." He took her arm. "Lawsuits are the last thing on my mind. I'm worried about Cody." His voice cracked on the last word.

"I shouldn't have said that." She pressed her fingers to her throbbing head. "I'm terrified and on edge."

"Understandably so." Having reached the end of the creek, he turned back, sweeping the light ahead of them, up along trees with branches fat and low enough for a child to climb. Owl eyes gleamed back at them. "Later we'll figure out if there's fault and if so, that employee will be dismissed. Right now we can only think about one thing."

"I appreciate that you're able to keep such a cool head." She swallowed down her fear and forced herself to think about the search for her son.

"You know, Stone and I wandered off once."

She realized he was likely trying to calm her by making aimless conversation, but she appreciated the effort, grounding herself in his deep steady voice. "Really? Where did you go?"

"Into these woods." His footsteps crunched as he backtracked toward the ranch again. "We planned to live off the land like cowboys, catch fish, build a fire and sleep in a tent."

"Obviously you made it home all right."

"A thunderstorm rolled through and drenched us. We got sick on the candy we packed, since we didn't catch a single fish." Flashlights from other searchers sent splashes of light through the trees, voices echoing. "And we had so many mosquito bites Gran made us wear gloves to keep from scratching."

"What gave you the idea to try such a dangerous thing?" she asked, on the off chance that would give her some insight to where her son might have wandered off to.

"We were boys. Boys don't need a reason to do stupid things," he said dryly.

"While I can agree on that," she answered with a much-needed smile, brief, then fading, "I think something made the two of you run off."

Alex sighed. "Stone's junkie mom had just threatened to take him again, and when I asked my parents to file for custody, they said no," he recounted with an emotionless voice at odds with his white-knuckled grip on the massive flashlight as they drew closer to the corrals. "Gran even asked them once too. But no go. Anyhow, that day, we decided for twenty-four hours we would be brothers."

His story touched her heart with a sense of family she'd never had, and while it didn't excuse his keeping secrets from her, she could sense the conflict he must have felt over the stocks and the ownership of a place that meant so much to him.

She leaned against the corral rail, her flashlight pointing downward. "Thank you. For trying to distract me while we search—"

Alex held up a hand. "Shhh…Nina. Listen."

She straightened, tipping her ears to catch sounds carried on the breeze, to parse through the people shouting for her son, the four-wheeler driving.

And puppies mewling.

She gasped. "Puppies. He's—"

"With the puppies," Alex finished, already sprinting toward the barn where the children had played with livestock.

Where he'd shown Cody the litter of puppies.

They'd checked here earlier and hadn't seen him. Could they have missed him? Or maybe he hadn't made his way here yet when they came through the first time?

Nina raced past him and yanked open the barn door. "Cody? Cody?"

Alex waved to her. "Over here. Asleep behind bales of hay holding a puppy."

She tore across the earthen floor, dropping to her knees and soaking in the sight of her son curled up around the fuzzy black puppy. He wasn't with all of the puppies. He just had one and they'd missed him. Somehow they'd overlooked him, but she wasn't going to second-guess. Not now. She was so damn grateful to have her child safe. Tears of relief streaked down her face, mixed with pent-up emotion from the entire week. She slid down to the ground, unable to escape reality.

She'd found her son—and now she needed to leave.

Eleven

Perched on the edge of Cody's bed, Nina tucked her son in for the night. He stared back at her as he rhythmically touched the top of his blanket, completely unconcerned. She should never have left him this evening. Shudders pulsated as her thoughts wandered on what could have happened. But Cody was here.

Safe.

She didn't take that gift of safety for granted for even an instant. This evening could have ended so horribly. She should be happy. Relieved. But she was still so shell-shocked by Alex's revelation and the hour of terror looking for her son that she could barely function. Nina let out a breath she didn't realize had been locked in her chest.

She smoothed Cody's hair and he let her touch him without flinching. "Please don't wander off without telling me, okay? I know it's difficult for you to talk, but this is important. I need to know where you are."

"Want that collie puppy," he whispered, and pulled a piece of paper from under his covers. He'd drawn a puppy playing in the barn. The detail was stunning, capturing the border collie perfectly. So much talent.

If only they'd found that picture earlier, it would have steered them right to him. "We'll get a puppy when we're home, okay, sweetie?"

Cody sat up, hugging his puffy blue blanket. He shook his head. "Want a puppy here."

Her heart tugged at all the things she couldn't give him. "Oh, my sweet boy, it's beautiful here and I love your pictures so very much. But we have to go home."

His eyes darted from side to side, stopping to stare at the outfit on his dresser. Fresh blue jeans sat beneath a brand-new yellow cowboy shirt. A brand-new kid-sized Stetson hat rested on the top of the pile. Pale tan rope circled the base of the hat, the ends joined by a silver horse charm. New brown cowboy boots with a matching fringe vest sat next to the clothes. "The wedding. I have new clothes. We gotta go to the wedding. With the kitty lady."

His jaw jutted.

She could see him ramping up and needed a way to calm him. "We'll go to the wedding. You will get to wear your new outfit."

"Okay, okay."

"But I need you to promise me you won't wander off like that again. You could have been hurt. I was very scared for you. I need you to say the words, Cody. Promise me."

He avoided her eyes, but he nodded, lying back down again. "Promise."

"Good boy." She patted the blue blanket. "It's time to go to sleep. Night-night. I love you so much."

She could speak multiple languages, but words were so hard to find to get through to her precious child. What would she have done tonight without Alex's support?

Ah, Alex. The heartbreaking cowboy. Now, there was a touchy subject. Her stomach tightened as her brain tried to make sense of her conflicting emotions.

Backing away from Cody's bed, she adjusted the Buckaroo Bronco lamp on her way out. She closed the door softly. Sagging back against the panel, she let the tears flow, wishing the pain could be uncorked so easily.

A movement deep in the living room snagged her attention and she saw Alex rise from the sofa. Had it only been a few hours ago he'd come here to take her to the party? She'd dressed with such hope and silly expectations from a tube of mascara.

He walked across the floor and wrapped his arms around her. She pushed against his chest in a half-hearted attempt to make some kind of point. To get back at him for seeming so perfect and being so very flawed. Even worse, dishonest. Was he really just another frog-prince?

Crying harder, she pressed her face against his chest to muffle the sounds so her son wouldn't hear. She twisted her hands in his shirt.

Her legs buckled and his arms banded tighter around her. He smoothed her hair and mumbled words against her head. He backed closer to the living area until he sat in the fat armchair and pulled her into his lap. She continued to cry, not the hard racking sobs anymore, but the silent slip of tears down her cheeks. His hands roved up and down her back rhythmically.

As she shifted, her face brushed his. Or maybe his brushed hers and their mouths met, held. She should pull away. This was a bad idea for a thousand reasons that would only lead to more heartache. But this was her last chance to feel his hands on her, his mouth. She didn't want lies, excuses or half-truths. She didn't even want to talk. She wanted this. This man might not have what she needed from life, but she would take this moment of pleasure for herself before she left. She'd come a long way from the woman who'd married Warren and hoped for the best.

She looped her arms around Alex's neck as she wriggled closer. Neither of them asked if it was right or wrong. Their bodies spoke, communed, and his hands clasped her hips, shifting her until she straddled his lap. He bunched her dress up, his fingers warm on her skin, twisting the thin barrier of her underwear until the strings along her hips *snapped*.

Without breaking their kiss she fished in his pocket for his wallet and found a condom. With sure hands she unbuckled that rodeo belt and unzipped his pants. He growled his approval against her mouth.

Then frenzy took over and she lowered herself onto him. Inch by inch. His hands on her hips, her hands on his shoulders and yes… Her head fell back as their hips rolled in sync. Faster and faster. The heat and need built inside her, all the pent-up emotion from the night, crushed dreams and disappointment leaving her raw.

Soon—too soon and yet not soon enough—she felt

the rise of her orgasm building, slamming through her, riding the wave of all those emotions. She sank her teeth in Alex's shoulder to keep from shouting out. His hands clenched in her hair, his fists tight as she felt his release rock through him.

In the aftermath, she kept her face tucked into his neck while he stroked her back. Even though she would be attending the wedding tomorrow, she knew…

This was goodbye.

Wedding photos and receiving line complete, Alex was finally free to mingle before dinner and dancing kicked into high gear. He knew more about weddings than most men. After all, the Hidden Gem hosted them on a regular basis. And he focused on every damn detail tonight to keep from thinking about the hole in his heart over losing Nina. Last night had put him through the emotional wringer—from their fight, to Cody wandering off, and then to making love with Nina in a frenzied moment that had goodbye written all over it.

Damn straight he needed to think of something else to keep from walking away to lose himself in a bottle of booze in the solitude of his suite. So he focused on every detail, making sure the wedding and reception went off without a hitch.

And damned if he wasn't too aware of Nina and Cody's presence anyway.

Even knowing she'd only attended because her son had been emphatic about it didn't stop the rush of pleasure having them here. The kid was something else. Who'd have thought he would dig his heels in on wearing his new clothes and attending a cowboy wedding? Cody looked as though he belonged here, at Hidden

Gem Ranch, with his cowboy outfit. Guilt struck at Alex, rattling through his chest. He had to focus.

The vows Johanna and Stone had spoken were from the heart, the ceremony in the chapel brief. One groomsman and one bridesmaid—Alex and Amie. The bride wore a simple fitted lace dress with a short train. The loose, romantic waves of her hair complemented the airiness of her dress. Elegant. Understated. Her lone bridesmaid wore a peach-colored dress in a similar but simpler style, to the floor without a train.

Stone and Alex wore tan suits with buff-colored Stetsons for when they were outside. This event was about the bride and groom, their style, making memories on their day.

At the end of the service, as Alex escorted his sister out of the church, he felt the weight of Nina's gaze, felt the hurt he'd caused her. More guilt. More shame. And he didn't know how the hell to make it right and he didn't know who to turn to for guidance.

Silently he and Amie walked to the barn where the rehearsal dinner had been held. All of the decorations from the night before were still in place, plus more. Gold chandeliers and puffs of white hydrangeas dangled from the barn rafters. Strings of lights crisscrossed the ceiling, creating an intimate, dreamy atmosphere. Bouquets of baby's breath and roses tied with burlap bows graced all the tables. The inside had been transformed into rustic elegance, with gold chairs and white tulle draped throughout.

There were rustic touches as well. At the entry table next to the leather guest book, seating cards were tied to horse shoes that had the bride and groom's names engraved along with the wedding date. A cowbell hung on a brass hook with a sign that stated Ring for a Kiss.

A country band played easy-listening versions of old classics.

But Alex was in no mood for dancing. Not if he couldn't have Nina in his arms. She'd made it clear last night after she'd booted him out of her bed that she was leaving right after the wedding. She'd only stayed this long for Cody. Alex poured himself a drink and found a table in the far back corner. Isolated. He would have to move up front with the family soon enough. For now, he could be alone with his drink and his thoughts.

"Mind if I join you?" His father stood beside him.

"Um, no, not at all." He gestured to an empty chair. "Have a seat, but Gran will insist we move up front to the main table soon."

"Then we might as well enjoy this as long as we can." Garnet tipped back his drink. "You look like you could use some support—or advice. Woman troubles?"

"There's nothing anyone can do." Alex sipped the bourbon, watching Nina and Cody talk to the bride. The little boy touched the bridal bouquet with reverence.

Memories of walking the ranch looking for Cody gut-kicked Alex all over again. He'd never known a fear that deep. Or a relief so intense once they'd found him.

Rattling the ice in his glass, Garnet followed Alex's gaze before studying his son hard. "People think your mother married me for my money and that I live off my inheritance. And they wouldn't be totally wrong on either of those points. But you know what, son?"

Alex met his father's piercing gaze—the McNair blue eyes—and finally saw a little of Gran in there. "What, Dad?"

"It's none of their damn business. Bayleigh and I may not live our lives the way others would, but it works for us." He thumbed his wedding ring around his finger. "We have a happy marriage. I did learn that from my parents. Pick the right person for you and to hell with everyone else's expectations. This is your life."

Alex wasn't sure how to apply the advice to his own personal hell, but he appreciated his father's effort. "Any reason you never thought to have this kind of father-son talk with me before now?"

"You didn't need it then." Garnet shrugged, adjusting his bolo tie. "Now I believe you do."

"It's not that simple with Nina." There. Alex had said it. Acknowledged that he and Nina were—or had been—a couple. He wanted her in his life.

"Sure it's every bit as simple as that. Buy the stocks from her. Pay more than they're worth and give that boy some extra security." Garnet's practicality sounded more and more like a McNair by the second. Maybe everyone had underestimated him. "So what if the ranch has to scrimp on mechanical bulls for a while? Big deal."

"You make it sound so easy." Very easy. Doable.

"Because it is." Garnet set aside his drink. "Your grandmother only said get the stocks back in the family. She didn't say who had to buy them. If you need me to chip in, consider it done."

And Alex could see his father meant it. He was offering to help. Alex clapped him on the shoulder, the advice solidifying in his mind with utter clarity. "Thanks, Dad. Really. But I think you already gave me what I needed most with your advice."

"Then what's holding you back?"

"I need for Gran to be at peace with this. Ever since I met Nina, it's stopped being about the ranch. It's about giving Gran peace."

His father nodded, gesturing to the front of the room where Gran held court with the bride, Amie—and Nina. Family. That was what meant the most to Gran.

This plan might not be what she'd had in mind, but his grandmother had always respected leadership and honor.

And love. There it was, no hiding from the truth anymore. Yes, it was impulsive and fast, but he'd never been so sure of anything in his life. Alex loved Nina. He loved her son as well, and he intended to do whatever it took to become their family.

Nina twisted her hands together, nervous at the attention from the McNair matriarch. Sweat began to build in her palms. Did the woman know her plans had been uncovered? Mariah was so fragile; it was easy to see how a person would do anything to make her final days as drama-free as possible.

Then again, damn it, if that had been the woman's goal, why come up with elaborate tests for her grandchildren to prove their loyalty to the family? Mariah's process of inheritance seemed to invite problems. Frustration simmered, balancing out the empathy. Nina's emotions were a huge mess today.

Mariah took Nina's hand in her cool grasp, her skin paper thin and covered with bruises from IVs. Despite her frailty, Mariah's grip was firm, confident. A true businesswoman. "I'm so glad your son was found safely."

"I appreciate all the help searching. This week has been a dream come true for him. I understand I have you to thank for getting him into the program."

Mariah's eyes went wide at Nina's frank approach—

and then she smiled sympathetically. "I'm sorry that life has to be so difficult for you."

"Life is hard for everyone in some way, ma'am. I love Cody. I have a good job in my field that allows me to stay home with my son. My life is good."

Life is good. This was what Nina had repeated over and over to herself as she dressed for the weekend. She desperately tried to convince herself that she didn't need anything else besides Cody and work. Tried to tell herself that was all she wanted. That it was enough.

"Then why are your eyes so sad?"

How could she tell the woman about the doomed affair with Alex? She couldn't. "My in-laws will use the incident with Cody getting lost to try and take him away from me. They think he would be better off in a hospital, coming home on holidays and weekends. And they want control of his inheritance from his father."

What was it about this woman that made Nina spill her secret fears?

"That has to be so incredibly frightening for you. They sound like they're using the issue of institutionalizing him as a power play."

Nina nodded. "They are." She looked at the deathly ill woman in front of her and saw complete clarity in her eyes. Nina didn't want to burden her, but honesty might allay Mariah's concerns about those stocks more than all this behind-the-scenes game playing. "Ma'am, with all due respect, if you wanted Cody's stocks, why didn't you just approach me and give me a chance to be a reasonable businesswoman?"

Mariah's pale blue eyes went wide and she gripped her cane. "So Alex has told you." She smiled, bringing color back to her pale face. "Good for him."

What? "I'm confused. You wanted to keep this a secret but you didn't?" Nina didn't appreciate having her life manipulated, regardless of how ill the older woman was.

"I want to apologize for bringing you here under false pretenses. My grandson is so introverted. He communes with the animals more than people, and that's a part of what makes him so successful at running the Hidden Gem. But he also needed a nudge outside his comfort zone. I hoped forcing a meeting between the two of you would help him move forward with having a life that doesn't center on work 24/7. Life's too short, too precious." Mariah leaned closer. "You must realize by now that the crush he had on Johanna was born more out of convenience than any real passion. When I see the two of you together—" her eyes twinkled with life "—now, that's passion."

How could Nina tell Mariah the test backfired? They'd broken up. He'd lied to her...for a few days. Then come clean. Could she forgive that? After her marriage, she had issues on that front, no question. But Alex had shown more compassion and honor in a week than her ex had displayed in their entire marriage.

Mariah squeezed Nina's hand and continued. "I took advantage of your desire to help your son. That was wrong of me."

"You were desperate to do anything for your family. I understand that feeling." As Nina said those words, she felt the truth of them settle deep in her soul. Life wasn't about black and white, right and wrong. It was about flawed humans doing their best, one day at time.

Now if she could just find a way to make Alex understand that her love for him was every bit as strong as her love for her son.

If he could understand that, they would be able to find a way to work through this tangle.

Together.

A box in his arms, Alex knocked on Nina's cabin door with his boot. Moonlight sparkled through the branches overhead. Now that he had his compass firmly planted, he'd accomplished a lot in a few short hours, busy as hell setting things into motion all while seeing his cousin off at the end of the wedding. But then a rancher was a multitasker by nature. He didn't want to waste another second. He had to win Nina over and keep her in his life.

Hopefully forever.

She opened the door, her hair wet from a shower, wearing pj shorts and a loose shirt. And she'd never looked more beautiful.

"Mind if I come in?"

She stepped back, opening the door wider to reveal packed suitcases by the sofa. Her vintage bag sported large stickers displaying sites from around the world. "We need to talk."

God, he hoped that was a good sign.

"Let's sit on the sofa. I have a few things to show you."

Her face gave nothing away as she padded silently beside him. Either she was egoing to boot him out on his butt. Or, if she somehow still had a shred of hope for their relationship, she was going to make him work for it.

Fine. Ranchers were well versed in hard work. He

was putting everything on the line tonight now that he knew exactly what he wanted.

"Nina, I realize I royally messed things up between us. I should have been honest from the start. I let my fear for my grandmother cloud my judgment, and that's the last thing she would want."

She rested a hand on his arm. "I understand—"

No way was he giving her a chance to let him down easy or tell him she'd already called a cab. He plowed ahead, situating the box he'd brought beside him. He needed to bring out everything he had. Now.

"I'm not sure that you do understand just how much you mean to me and how much I value the woman you are, but I'm hoping this will show you." He reached into the box and pulled out a book. "This is from the family library. It contains the French poem I gave you on our first date."

He set the leather-bound edition on her coffee table.

She traced the gold lettering on the front. "I thought you looked up the poem on the internet."

He would have laughed at that if he wasn't still scared out of his mind she had one foot out the door already. "That certainly would have been faster. But the journey is well worth the effort."

Next, he pulled out a box of Swiss chocolates and a Violet Crumble candy bar from Australia. "These came from our gift shop, but they're just a sampling of places I want to take you and Cody. I know you've given up a lot of dreams for your son, Nina, and I'd like to give them back to you. I want to ride in the Swiss Alps with you and make love under the stars. I want to take Cody to Australia and show him a whole other kind of cowboy to enjoy."

He meant it too. He'd stuck close to home ever since leaving the rodeo circuit, finding peace at the Hidden Gem. But he wanted to see more of the world through Nina's eyes.

Her hands went to her heart, but she stayed silent.

"I also want Cody to learn to love the ranch here."

"He already does," she said softly.

"Good, but I want him to feel a part of the history of this place." He pulled out a heavy woven blanket. "This is a Native American blanket made by one of our local artisans, quite heavy, and I thought it might be of comfort to Cody. And even if the blanket doesn't suit him, I want this to be a symbol of how much I care for your son."

Tears welled in her eyes as she took the blanket from him and clasped it her chest. "Alex, you don't need to say any more. You've already—"

He touched her lips to quiet her, hoping maybe he was getting through to her. But he had a lot to make up for and he wasn't taking any chances on screwing this up too.

"I worked to pull this together tonight and intend to see it through because it's important to me that you know how much you mean to me, Nina." Deep inside the box, he withdrew a manila envelope. "This contains the proposal my investment broker just sent to yours."

She took the envelope and pulled out the papers, her hands trembling. She scanned the documents, then gasped. "Oh my God, Alex. Why did you offer to pay such a ridiculous amount for Cody's stocks? I thought you said your cash flow was tied up right now?"

"I did this because it's the right thing to do," he answered simply. "Cody is an amazing kid. I hope with every fiber of my being that with you as his advocate, he will have a future full of independence. But I know that's not a given. So I did what I could to help him."

She cocked her head to the side. "You really did risk your inheritance by pursuing me instead of taking your grandmother's 'test.' You're not trying to buy me off?"

As if that could even be done? He knew her better than that. This was a woman with deep values and a huge heart. "Nina, I would do just about anything for you. But this was for Cody, because that boy has come to mean a lot to me. Because I want the best for his future too."

A future Alex hoped he would be a part of.

She tucked the papers back into the envelope and set them on top of the blanket. "You didn't put your own finances at risk for this, did you?"

"I'll be fine. Hidden Gem will be fine. It's a done deal." His grandmother was ecstatic. Now he just prayed it was enough to keep Nina and Cody in his life.

She smoothed her hand along the envelope. "I don't know what to say to that other than thank you."

He rested his hand over hers. "You could say you forgive me."

She drew in a shaky breath. "I wish you could have been open with me from the beginning, and especially as we got to know each other, but I can understand how deeply torn you must have felt the effects of your grandmother's illness."

"You're too forgiving." His hands slid up her arms as he started to hope this could work out after all. "I have one more thing for you in the box. Are you still interested?"

She smiled. "Most definitely."

God, how crazy that he was nervous over this part when he knew with every fiber of his being it was exactly what he wanted. But then nothing had ever been this important. He reached in to pull out a dozen yellow roses.

"I know that red roses are supposed to signify love, but we're in Texas, and the yellow rose is our flower. I very much want you to be my Texas rose. Now. Always. Because in spite of my quiet tendency to keep to myself, I have fallen impulsively, totally in love with you, Nina Lowery."

The tears in her eyes spilled over and she launched into his arms, the flowers crushing between them and releasing sweet perfume.

Her mouth met his and she kissed him once, twice and again, before pulling back. "Oh God, Alex, I love you too. Your strength, your tenderness, the way you always put others first, which makes me want to be your champion, giving back to you the way you give to so many others."

His heart pounded with relief and happiness. How did he get this damn lucky? "I have a plan. We can see each other every week while we work out details. If you don't want to move I can look into opening a Hidden Gem in San Antonio."

She gasped. "You would do that for me?"

"For you, absolutely." He cupped her face in his hands. "I want what's best for you and Cody. We can figure that out together."

She set aside the crushed flowers and pulled out one long-stemmed bud that had survived. "Actually my job enables me to live anywhere. So I was thinking more along the lines of a long-term rental of one of the cabins. You and I could...date." She trailed the flower under her nose and then provocatively between her breasts. "Get to know each other better. Turn this fling into an all-out affair."

"Ah," he sighed, anticipation pumping through him. "I can romance you. Win you over."

"You've already won me over. Lock, stock and barrel, I'm yours." She traced a rosebud along the side of his face. "And *you* are mine."

* * * * *

*If you loved Alex's romance,
pick up the other books in
USA TODAY bestselling author
Catherine Mann's
DIAMONDS IN THE ROUGH series:*

*Stone's story
ONE GOOD COWBOY
Available now from Harlequin Desire!*

and

*Amie's story
PREGNANT BY THE COWBOY CEO
Available July 2015 from Harlequin Desire!*

*If you're on Twitter, tell us what you think of
Harlequin Desire! #harlequindesire*

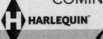

COMING NEXT MONTH FROM

HARLEQUIN

Desire

Available July 7, 2015

#2383 THE BILLIONAIRE'S DADDY TEST
Moonlight Beach Bachelors • by Charlene Sands
Mia D'Angelo will not turn over her niece to the baby's unsuspecting father until she knows the reclusive billionaire is daddy material. But when Adam Chase uncovers her ruse, he's ready to make his own very personal demands...

#2384 SEDUCED BY THE SPARE HEIR
Dynasties: The Montoros • by Andrea Laurence
When black-sheep Prince Gabriel unexpectedly finds himself in line to the throne, he turns to Serafia Espina to revamp his image. But when they go from friends to lovers, a family secret resurfaces, threatening everything they've begun.

#2385 PREGNANT BY THE COWBOY CEO
Diamonds in the Rough • by Catherine Mann
Amie McNair spent one impulsive night with the McNair empire's new CEO, Preston Armstrong. Now she's pregnant! Can she keep her secret when they must travel—in close quarters—on a two-week cross-country business trip?

#2386 LONE STAR BABY BOMBSHELL • by Lauren Canan
It isn't until *after* their one-night stand that Kelly realizes Jace isn't just a handsome cowboy—he's an award-winning actor and a notorious playboy. Now that he's back in town, how will she tell him he's a father?

#2387 CLAIMING HIS SECRET SON
The Billionaires of Black Castle • by Olivia Gates
Billionaire Richard Graves escaped from his mercenary past years ago, but he still wants his enemy's widow for himself. When their lives collide again, can he let go of old wounds despite the secret she's been keeping?

#2388 A ROYAL AMNESIA SCANDAL • by Jules Bennett
After her royal boss's accident, assistant Kate Barton must pretend to be the fiancée he doesn't remember leaving. But soon her romantic role becomes all too real. How will she explain her pregnancy when his memory returns?

YOU CAN FIND MORE INFORMATION ON UPCOMING HARLEQUIN® TITLES, FREE EXCERPTS AND MORE AT WWW.HARLEQUIN.COM.

HDCNM06

Gabriel took another step toward her, closing in on her personal space. With her back pressed against the oak armoire, she had no place to go. A part of her didn't really want to escape anyway. Not when he looked at her like that.

His dark green eyes pinned her in place, and her breath froze in her lungs. He wasn't just trying to flatter her. He did want her. It was very obvious. But it wasn't going to happen for an abundance of reasons that started with his being the future king and ended with his being a notorious playboy. Even dismissing everything in between, it was a bad idea. Serafia had no interest in kings or playboys.

"Well, I'll do my best to not annoy you, but I do so enjoy the flush across your cheeks and the sparkle in your dark eyes. My gaze is drawn to the rise and fall of your breasts as you breathe harder." He took another step closer. Now he could touch her if he chose. "If you don't want me to make you angry anymore, I could think of another way to get the same reaction that would be more...*pleasurable* for us both."

Serafia couldn't help the soft gasp that escaped her lips
at his bold words. For a moment, she wanted to pull him
hard against her. Every nerve in her body buzzed from his
closeness. She felt the heat of his body radiating through
the thin silk of her blouse. Her skin flushed and tightened
in response.

One palm reached out and made contact with the
polished oak at her back. He leaned in and his cologne
teased at her nose with sandalwood and leather. The com-
bination was intoxicating and dangerous. She could feel
herself slipping into an abyss she had no business slipping
into. She needed to stop this before it went too far. Serafia
was first and foremost a professional.

"I'm not sleeping with you," she blurted out.

Gabriel's mouth dropped open in mock outrage.
"Miss Espina, I'm shocked."

Serafia chuckled, the laughter her only release for
everything building up inside her. She arched one eyebrow. "Shocked that I would be so blunt or shocked that
I'm turning you down?"

He smiled and her knees softened beneath her.

"Shocked that you would think that was all I wanted
from you."

*Don't miss SEDUCED BY THE SPARE HEIR
by Andrea Laurence, part of the*
DYNASTIES: THE MONTOROS series:

*MINDING HER BOSS'S BUSINESS by Janice Maynard
CARRYING A KING'S CHILD by Katherine Garbera
SEDUCED BY THE SPARE HEIR by Andrea Laurence
THE PRINCESS AND THE PLAYER by Kat Cantrell
MAID FOR A MAGNATE by Jules Bennett
A ROYAL TEMPTATION by Charlene Sands*

Only from Harlequin® Desire
www.Harlequin.com